BLISTER

JEFF STRAND

CHAPTER ONE

I'm a liar, but this is the truth.

I may let this messed up tale be published after I'm dead. Or I may not. I haven't decided yet. Right now it's just for me.

If it does get published, I want to assure you that I wrote every word of this. I'm saying that because you probably assumed that they paid some ghostwriter, or that it's one of those "as told to _____" deals where I babbled into a tape recorder and somebody organized my thoughts into something coherent and marketable. It's not. These are my words on the page. My blood on the keyboard.

I'm Jason Tray. Yes, that Jason Tray. You may already know what happened. I'd prefer that you didn't—preconceptions are a bitch. But no matter what you've seen, heard, or read, it's not the complete truth. This is. Warts and all. If you're looking for warts, trust me, I've got some lovely witch-warts for you to gape at in these pages, ladies and gentlemen!

Don't worry, I promise this isn't going to be some whiny "Oh, alas, poor, poor innocent me!" string of excuses that makes you want to shove a few fingers down your throat. I'm not looking for posthumous pity. I just want to make a record of exactly what happened, and why it happened.

I'm writing this in 1986, but for the events themselves we've got to rewind back to September of 1985, where my little story begins with two of the neighborhood kids. Greg and Dennis. School had started a couple of weeks ago, and one afternoon I looked out of my living room window and saw them standing outside of my backyard, rattling the metal links on the fence to rile up my Schnauzer. No big deal. I'd taunted a dog or two when I was ten. I went back to work.

The next day, they did the same thing. Ignatz ran back and forth, barking furiously, while the kids laughed and shouted things including but not limited to "You can't get me, you stupid dog!" Though I couldn't argue the truth of their assessment of his intelligence (Ignatz was the sweetest dog I'd ever owned, but his brain capacity was low), I decided to put a stop to this.

I came out the back door and gave them a friendly smile. "Hey, I'm gonna have to ask you guys not to tease my dog. The people next door get upset if he barks too much."

Greg gave me the finger. "Screw you, old man!" The kids ran off, laughing.

Old man? *Old man?* I was thirty-eight! *Barely* thirty-eight; I'd just celebrated a birthday last month. Little bastards. I played fetch with Ignatz for a few minutes, then took him inside and resumed drawing the day's installment of *Off Balance*, the comic strip I'd been doing for the past decade. The punchline to this particular strip involved Zep the Beetle having a stone gargoyle shoved up his nose, which was proving to be a more difficult artistic challenge than I'd anticipated.

On the third day, the rotten brats threw rocks. I made it outside just in time to hear a loud yip as a rock hit Ignatz in the side. Greg and Dennis ran away. Ignatz didn't seem hurt—he licked my face happily as I scooped him into my arms—but it was time to involve the parents.

If I remembered correctly, Greg's house was the red one on the corner, two blocks down. I put Ignatz inside, walked over there, and knocked on the door. A tired-looking, heavyset blonde woman answered.

"Hi," I said. "Are you Greg's mother?"

"Yes."

"I'm Jason Tray, I live in the white house about two—"

"The one with the graveyard in the front yard?"

I smiled. "Only at Halloween."

She didn't smile back. "All of October, actually."

"Right. Anyway, your son and his friend were throwing rocks at my dog."

"Maybe they were defending themselves."

"He's inside a fence."

"Maybe they were worried that it was going to get out."

I shook my head. "If they were worried he was going to get out, they wouldn't stand there and throw rocks at him. Look, I'm not one of those 'Hey you kids, get off my lawn!' neighbors."

"Uh-huh."

"Seriously, I'm not. I just can't have your son hurting my dog. So if you could have a talk with him and let him know that it's not cool to throw things at animals, I'd appreciate it."

"Why don't you keep it inside?"

"The whole reason I've got a fence is so Ignatz can be outside. I'm not asking you to keep your kid indoors; I'm asking you to tell him to quit behaving like a psychopath."

I cringed at my own comment, since parents tended to react

poorly when you referred to their child as a psychopath. But this lady was starting to piss me off.

Greg's mother barely even acknowledged my comment. She sort of nodded and sort of shrugged. I stood there for a moment, waiting for a verbal response.

"Thanks," I finally said, figuring that the conversation was over.

"Okay."

I walked back to my house. I'd been tempted to mention that her ten-year-old son was giving the finger to adults, but I didn't want to be a whiny tattletale. As long as they weren't destroying stuff or harming pets, I was fine with kids being kids. I'd lived in this neighborhood for nearly three years without any problems.

The next day, I was so absorbed in my work that I didn't realize what time it was until I heard Ignatz yelp in pain. I rushed out the door just as those little shits each threw another rock at him through the fence, both of which missed. They ran off, laughing. I crouched down next to Ignatz and ran my fingers through his fur. There was a small welt on his back.

Now, I realize that I was the mature adult and they were the children, and that I should have taken the higher road. But I wasn't in a "higher road" kind of mood. I drew fast and was way ahead of deadline on *Off Balance*, and that made it very easy for me to take the rest of the day off to plot my revenge.

First, I needed a fake chainsaw. Not some cheap rubber thing— I wanted one that looked and sounded totally real, but wouldn't actually, y'know, slice children in half. After a few phone calls, I found one at a costume shop that was an hour and a half away. I enjoyed the drive.

I wanted to find a phony severed head that looked as if it could belong to a ten-year-old, but I wasn't able to locate one that I could get by the following afternoon. So I went with an adult head—a really cool one with a rubber tongue lolling out of its mouth and part of the spinal column dangling from its neck.

The next day, I let Ignatz out into the yard and splashed some fake blood on my face and clothes. I looked at myself in the mirror. Nope, not enough. By the time I was satisfied, I was absolutely *drenched* in gore. Heh heh.

The reprehensible little creeps showed up on schedule. As Dennis pounded his fist against the fence, I burst out of the door and ran toward them, a severed head in my right hand, a roaring chainsaw in my left.

Greg and Dennis shrieked. The crotch of Greg's pants immediately darkened. They fled, screaming in terror.

Yeah, I know. I really should have left it at that. Instead, I opened the gate and chased them down the sidewalk, letting out my most maniacal laugh, which I was disappointed they wouldn't be able to hear over the chainsaw, since it was a pretty darn freaky laugh.

At the end of the block, Dennis fell, landing hard. Greg just left his friend and continued running toward his house, never looking back.

I shut off the chainsaw and walked over to Dennis. He'd wet his pants, too. And his arm was bent at a funny angle.

Oops.

I had a feeling that this was going to create some problems in my life.

"Why?" asked Chuck Rhodes, my agent and publicist, sitting across from me in the upscale seafood restaurant where he always ordered barbecue ribs. "Why would you think it was okay to chase after young children with a chainsaw in broad daylight?"

"It was a *faux* chainsaw."

"Don't be a smartass. This isn't funny."

"A lot of people would disagree with you. I should do a strip about it."

"Jason, I'm serious. Just because the parents didn't press charges doesn't mean they won't sue. This could be an absolute nightmare."

"You're supposed to enjoy this stuff."

"No. No, I'm not." Chuck took a big gulp of his ice water. The poor guy was in his mid-forties but looked ten years older. He often tried to blame those extra ten years on me, although since he had six teenagers (three adopted) I refused to accept responsibility for his totally gray hair and plentiful wrinkles.

"I already said I'm paying for his doctor's bill. I'll even draw a few cartoons on his cast."

"Yeah, that makes up for it. Those kids could be traumatized for life."

"So they go through life with a fear of lunatics carrying severed heads and chainsaws. They *should* be scared. My chainsaw was fake, but the next one they encounter might not be."

"Again, not funny. Not funny at all. The fifteen through nineteen demographic might be amused by your little stunt, but most other age groups don't approve of people who break the arms of children. You could lose papers over this."

"It'll be fine," I said. "We'll make sure a really adorable photo of Ignatz goes out to the media and everybody will be on my side."

Chuck sighed. "You know, Festering Pus doesn't give me any problems. Why is it that the heavy metal band doesn't create any headaches in my life, but the cartoonist does? Did you know that they leave hotel rooms in better shape than when they got there? It's true. They leave flowers for housekeeping. But you drive me crazy. Legitimately insane."

"Sorry."

Chuck was hugely responsible for my career success, though if I'd known what the hell I was doing when I first tried to break in as a cartoonist, I probably never would've signed with him. Like me, he lived in Jacksonville, Florida, instead of working out of New York City, and he represented all manner of clients in all manner of ways, with virtually no area of specialty. But he worked incredibly hard, was a good friend, and I never thought of switching to a "real" agent, even when big names came calling. On the other hand, I'm sure there were plenty of times when he felt like giving me the boot.

Off Balance took off faster than anybody ever expected, and some money started to pour in. That's when I found out that I've got money guilt. I thought I had chrematophobia, but it turns out that's an actual *fear* of money, which is even weirder than my problem. When I received my first really big check, I felt sick to my stomach. Why should I be making this much for sitting at home drawing funny pictures? So I started writing checks to various charities. I did it quietly—this wasn't one of those mega-celebrity "Look at me! Look at me! I gave .0007% of my yearly income to this worthy cause!" deals.

Oddly enough, the IRS questioned the idea that I donated almost all of my income to charity. This led to some problems as I had to prove that I wasn't funneling my money to fund terrorism or something like that. Fortunately, I may have financial guilt issues, but I'm not (too) stupid, and I kept all my receipts. It then became a minor news story—the wacky successful cartoonist who gives away all his cash.

Of course, I was made out to be some nutcase living behind a Dumpster, licking dried nougat from discarded candy bar wrappers for sustenance. Chuck didn't like this. He also didn't like it when, as a result of this publicity, he got flooded with literally thousands of requests for "donations." So instead of That Weirdo Who's Ashamed of His Income, I suddenly became That Stingy Bastard Who Wouldn't Give Me Money To Remodel My Home. I tried to just keep my head down and focus on my work.

Until I organized a letter-writing campaign against a few newspapers that censored my weeklong series of strips where Zep thought he found God living in his goldfish aquarium. Chuck didn't like me doing that. Neither did my editor. But I thought the strips were funny and harmless. In retrospect, I really shouldn't have started the campaign (which was, I must say, quite successful) but, hey, I was angry.

I also threw a cherry Slurpee at a reporter who asked me if Charles Schultz's influence on the world of cartooning was overrated. That wasn't so cool, I guess.

And I suppose there were other incidents, but that's not what I'm here to write about. Overall, I think the past couple of years had gone fairly smoothly, until that one time when I covered myself with fake blood and chased some kids with a chainsaw.

"You need a vacation," Chuck told me. "Just escape from everything for a while. The stress is getting to you."

"I'm really not under that much stress," I said.

"Well, *I'm* under stress, and it stresses me out even more to think that your dumb ass might talk to journalists. I'm sending you to my cabin."

"The one in Georgia?"

"No, the one in Iran. How many cabins do you think I own? I want you to drive up there and stay for a couple of weeks until all this blows over, or until you get your goddamn subpoena."

"I don't like cabins."

"Do you know what I don't give? A shit. Stay up there and catch some fish. Just stay out of my face while I try to clean up your mess."

"All right, all right, I'll go." Hanging out on a lake for a few days actually sounded like fun. It might provide the inspiration for some cabin-themed strips. "Just between you and me, though—the kid breaking his arm *was* kind of funny, wasn't it?"

Chuck just glared at me.

CHAPTER TWO

It took about two days for cabin fever to set in. This surprised me, because it wasn't as if Chuck's cabin was even a real cabin. It had a big-screen television with a satellite dish, a fully stocked bar, and a pinball machine. The only inconvenience was that the hot water in the shower ran out after about five minutes, and if I'd known that prior to lathering up, I could have prepared accordingly.

I did some fishing the first day, while Ignatz happily splashed around near the shore. I didn't know what kind of lure worked best in this lake, so I went through Chuck's tackle box and just picked the biggest one. After an hour of no bites, I switched to a flashy orange one that seemed to have twelve different moving parts. I gave up on that one after my second cast. The third lure was stolen from me by the thick underwater weeds, at which point I decided that fishing was not having the desired calming effect.

Kayaking worked, though. I must've been out there for nearly three hours, slowly gliding along the lake's surface, enjoying the peace and solace. I peered down into the clear water and watched hundreds of fish that had avoided my attempts at capture. Oh, sure, I still chuckled to myself every time I remembered the expression on those demon kids' faces when I burst out of my back door, but the serenity of the lake made me wonder if I really *had* been stressed out and ready to snap and simply not realized it.

The cabin had a microwave and a convection oven, but I decided to rough it and make a campfire. Dinner consisted of burnt hot dogs, burnt marshmallows, and way too many sour cream and onion-flavored potato chips.

But by the evening of the second day I started to get antsy. Which is ironic, because the life of a cartoonist pretty much just involves sitting at home, being anti-social. Not a lot of human contact. Still, I felt this incredible need to get out and socialize, so I brought Ignatz inside and then drove to a small bar about five miles from the cabin, which had caught my eye because the real sign was covered by a handwritten banner that said "Doug's Booze Wasteland."

There were about six people in the bar, all guys. It was not a tidy place.

"Somebody messed with your sign," I told the bartender, as I sat down on a stool.

He nodded. "Been that way for the past two years. It was a prank, but business improved after it went up, so I left it."

"Fair enough." I ordered a beer and looked around. Two guys were seated at a table, having an animated discussion, while two kids in their early twenties played pool. An old man sat alone in a booth, drinking hard liquor and looking depressed. I eavesdropped on the table conversation for a moment until I realized that it was about Reagan, then took my beer and approached the billiards table.

"Can I play the winner?" I asked.

"Sure thing," said the first kid, who wore a baseball cap and a plain blue t-shirt. He missed a ridiculously easy shot and cursed under his breath.

"I'm Jason Tray," I said, shaking both of their hands.

"Jason Tray...Jason Tray..." The second kid frowned. "Why does that sound familiar?"

"Do you read the daily comics?"

"Nah, the only good one is Garfield. Jason Tray...Jason Tray...oh, I know, you're Susan's new boyfriend. The zookeeper."

"Sorry, no."

A quick round of introductions and small talk let me know that I was hanging out with Louie and Erik, both of whom worked at an auto repair shop. Erik was on the prowl for hot chicks, and Louie was unhappily engaged. I explained my romantic situation, which involved a marriage at twenty-one and a divorce at twenty-nine, followed by several years of occasional but never serious girlfriends. My last one was six months ago. Penny. I broke up with her because I thought she never seemed to have time for me, and she happily accepted the breakup because she'd been seeing at least three other guys the entire time we were dating.

"I need another beer," said Louie, missing another easy shot.

"This round's on me." I ordered a couple more beers and handed them out, winning instant friends. Louie and Erik both continued to suck at pool as they outpaced my drinking by about three-to-one. An hour later, they were sloshed and I was buzzed as I tried unsuccessfully to explain some of my funnier comic strips, which are never funny when I describe them.

(Example: There's one where Zep the Beetle is at the dentist, who is explaining the stages of tooth decay using wind-up chattery teeth. If you've seen the strip, you know that it's hilarious, right? But it's mostly about the way I drew the teeth, especially the one with the worm.)

"We should go do something else," said Erik. "We need to find some women."

"Holly won't like that," said Louie.

"So? I'm not gonna tell her." Erik looked at me, or at least in my general direction. "Are you gonna tell her?"

"I don't even know her."

"See? Let's go find some skanks."

Louie shook his head. "Holly doesn't like me spending time with skanks. She gets all upset and stuff. When she's upset, it's like, no fun. We should go bowling."

"I'm not drunk enough for bowling," said Erik. "We should play darts."

Louie's face lit up. "Oh! Oh! You know what we should do? I know what we should do!"

"What?"

"We should take him to see Blister!"

Erik grinned. "Yeah! That'll be great! Way better than bowling."

"What's Blister?" I asked. It didn't sound appealing.

Louie started to answer, but Erik waved a hand in his face. "No, no, no, don't tell him. Let it be a surprise."

"I'm not big on surprises from really drunk guys," I admitted.

"It's cool," Erik assured me. "You'll love it. I'll drive."

"Yeah, right. You're not driving anywhere," I told him.

"Sure I am." He called out to the bartender. "Hey, Doug, can I have my keys?"

"Hell no."

"Do you want to drive?" Erik asked me.

"You guys aren't puking in *my* car."

Erik shrugged. "I guess we'll walk. It's not too far."

And so I found myself walking along a dirt road in the moonlight with a pair of intoxicated hooligans fifteen years younger than me. I wasn't buzzed enough for this to seem like a good idea, but I had just enough alcohol in my system to go along with it with only moderate protest. Louie and Erik staggered ahead, singing various popular hits that would be forever ruined for me.

"How much further?" I asked, after we'd been walking for about half an hour.

"Not much," Louie said.

"Are you lying to me?"

Louie stopped walking and considered that. "I don't think so."

"We should head back."

"Are you scared?"

"I'm scared of our stupidity," I said. "There's no way you're taking me someplace I'd want to go if I hadn't been drinking."

"It'll be worth it. I promise."

We resumed our walk. I really hoped that Louie and Erik weren't leading me toward anything illegal. Somehow I didn't see Chuck being cheerful about the whole situation if I got arrested.

It took another hour for us to reach our destination, although that included a fifteen-minute detour for Erik to unsuccessfully try to prove that he could climb a tree without using his arms. Finally, we stood at the end of the driveway of a small brown house, mostly hidden by woods with no other homes in the vicinity.

It was sort of run-down, with no lawn and an old silver pickup truck parked in front. A rocking chair on the front porch was missing the left runner. The windows were dark.

On the far side of the house, maybe fifty feet away, there was a wooden shed, about the size of a one-car garage.

"C'mon," Louie whispered, tugging on my arm.

I didn't move. "Whose house is this?"

"It doesn't matter. Let's go see Blister."

"Okay, I'm going to have to be the responsible adult here. I won't be doing any trespassing tonight, sorry."

"Suit yourself." Louie headed toward the house. Erik followed him.

I stood there, watching them. This whole thing was a bad idea on every conceivable level. That's why I rarely drank—it made me do dumb shit like this.

My intoxicated buddies walked past the house, toward the shed. Louie turned back and gestured for me to join them, at which point my still-buzzed brain decided that despite my intense reservations, I was legitimately curious about the whole Blister thing. I hurried down the driveway, mentally cursing myself with each step.

The shed had a small window. A light was on inside.

"Does somebody actually live in there?" I asked.

Louie and Erik shushed me. We crept closer to the shed, moving with exaggerated (and clumsy) stealth. Erik caught the giggles for a moment, so we waited for him to get over it, and then proceeded forward.

"Look in the window," Louie whispered.

"Uh-uh."

"Do it."

Slowly, carefully, I walked over to the shed. The shed was actually in much nicer condition than the house itself. It was hard to tell in the dark, but it looked to have been recently painted. For some reason I found this kind of creepy. Perhaps the shed was in better shape because it was where the owner of the house stored his precious tools and victims. Perhaps he liked to spend leisurely evenings with a tied-up woman and a hacksaw. Perhaps he was in there right now, cackling softly and gently kissing her forehead as he very, very slowly pulled the saw back and forth.

I hoped that wasn't it. I only enjoyed phony decapitations.

There was a knot in my stomach and my mind kept saying "Get the hell out of here!" but I was only a few feet away, and a quick glimpse inside couldn't hurt. I'd satisfy my curiosity, get Louie and

Erik off my back, and return to the cabin for some fishing. Maybe I'd try live bait instead of the metal lures. Yeah, that might work better.

I was scared.

I can't explain it. Obviously, there was the rational fear of getting caught—that made perfect sense. But there was another level of fear; the fear that what lurked inside that shed might not simply be a vision to amuse drunkards, but something *awful.*

My hands were sweaty and I wiped them off on my shirt.

I felt like a million eyes were watching me from within the woods. I wanted to turn and run away from the shed and the house as fast as I could.

But, no, I was right there, and I had to see. I was being silly. There were no killers or corpses in there.

I walked up to the side of the shed, then cautiously approached the window and peeked inside.

Somebody *did* live in there. I could see a neatly made bed in the corner, a small television, and an overflowing bookshelf. The wall was covered with pictures of owls, everything from crude drawings to photo-realistic paintings. The light came from an uncovered bulb dangling from the ceiling.

So the rickety old shed had been converted into a guesthouse. Still, what exactly was I supposed to see here? I was pretty sure it wasn't the owls.

Then with a sick feeling I realized what this must be about. No doubt the occupant of the shed liked to walk around naked. I was a frickin' peeping tom.

Oh, Chuck would love that. I could hear him shouting now: "You're not supposed to peek into people's windows after dark, you ridiculous idiot! I don't care how nice the breasts were!"

A face appeared.

I don't know how else to describe it except that it was...*horrible.*

Burnt and scarred and, except for its long blonde hair, barely recognizable as human. A God-awful mess. A monster.

I jumped back in shock. "*What the fuck is that..?*"

The thing in the shed let out a soft sob and disappeared from the window.

I hurried away as Louie and Erik fell to their knees and howled with laughter. Once I made it back to the road, they stumbled after me, still laughing. I quickly walked back the way we came, hoping to get far enough from the house that I wouldn't be seen if somebody came out to investigate. Louie and Erik rushed to catch up with me.

"What was that thing?" I demanded.

"What thing?" Erik put a hand over his mouth to stifle a giggle.

"Seriously, don't screw with me. What was that? Was that Blister?"

"It sure was," said Louie.

"That was fucked up. Don't do that again." Furious, I stormed back in the direction of the bar, wishing desperately that I could un-see that grotesque sight.

CHAPTER THREE

Despite not having been all *that* drunk, I woke up with a brain-crushing headache. At least I was in the appropriate bed and alone. I got up, took a four minute and fifty second shower, then got dressed and poured myself a glass of orange juice.

God, what a hideous face.

The best Louie and Erik could tell me was that Blister was "the town freak." Then they got distracted with butchering more perfectly good songs. We parted ways back at Doug's Booze Wasteland, where Doug called them a cab but I passed the Breathalyzer test he kept under the counter. I drove back to the cabin and went to bed.

My headache faded a bit as I kayaked on the lake, though the experience wasn't as relaxing this time. Maybe I just wasn't an outdoors kind of guy. Or maybe I should buy a container of nightcrawlers and do some more fishing. I'd promised Chuck that I'd lay low for at least a week, and I didn't want any blood vessels in his head to pop out and thrash around like cobras, so I decided to stick it out and get the worms.

I drove into "town" (which consisted of about six places of business) and went into the grocery store/tackle shop. I took a small plastic tub of worms out of a refrigerator that also contained a variety of carbonated beverages and brought it up to the front counter.

"Doing some fishing?" asked the cashier. He had a full white beard and looked about seventy.

"Yeah."

"Just making sure. You look like a worm-eater to me."

It took me a moment to realize that he was joking. I chuckled —usually I was one making jokes that people didn't get. "I gave that up earlier this year. Lost twelve pounds since then."

"Ah, I see. That explains it, then."

I paid for the tub and started to leave, then hesitated. "Hey, weird question for you. What do you know about Blister?"

His smile broadened, exposing a rotten tooth on the left side. "I'll bet you're not asking about the things you get on your hands and feet."

"Nope."

"Every town needs a spooky legend, don't you think? Blister's ours. Her father keeps her locked out back, never lets her out. I haven't seen her in years. She may even be dead. Be an act of mercy if she was."

"What happened to her?"

"Well, some folks say that her mother was a witch, and that on the night she was born—at the stroke of midnight—she ate her way out of her mother's womb. The child's skin was deformed, like she was filled with evil bubbling just under the surface, trying to rupture the flesh and spill out."

I just stared at him.

"That's horseshit, of course," he said with a laugh. "Hang out here long enough and you'll hear a dozen more versions of the Blister story. Truth is, she had a fight with her boyfriend. Nobody knows what caused it, but I think she was a bit too wholesome for him, if you know what I mean. He tied her down and went at her face with a straight razor and a blowtorch. Can you believe that? A blowtorch."

"Jesus."

"Yeah. He ruined her face, all right. I saw it once, and it made me just about sick to my stomach. I'd rather eat that tub of worms you bought than see it again."

The bell above the door rang as another customer entered. The cashier looked down at the counter, as if he'd been caught gossiping in class by the teacher. I thanked him and left.

So I was vacationing in a town where some nutcase kept his disfigured daughter locked up in a shed. And Chuck was pissed at *my* behavior.

But as I drove back to the cabin, I realized that I felt like...well, like a complete jerk. Not simply embarrassed because I'd acted like a drunken high school student, but ashamed of my cruel behavior. If the cashier's story was true—and admittedly, I had my doubts— then Blister had a pretty miserable life, and the last thing she needed was to have idiots like me peeking through her window saying, "What the fuck is that?"

Sure, it was pretty much all Louie and Erik's fault, but still...

I kept thinking about the sob she let out after I peeked in the window. What had it been? A sob of humiliation?

I needed to apologize.

Yep, just like the time I was twelve and I broke Mr. Scott's car window with a BB gun, I needed to suck it up, march over there, knock on the front door, and say that I was sorry. And I needed to do it now, before I convinced myself that it wasn't important and it became a small but ferocious bit of guilt gnawing away at me after I returned home.

Actually, there was something I needed to do at the cabin first. But immediately after that, I was going to drive back to the brown house in the woods with the shed and apologize to Blister.

A MAN SAT on the front porch as I pulled into the driveway. He was seated in the broken rocking chair, smoking a cigarette. He stared at me suspiciously as I turned off the engine and got out of my car, a rolled-up sheet of paper tucked under my arm.

"Hi there," I said.

He nodded, but it wasn't in a friendly manner. "Hi."

I walked up onto the porch. The knot in my stomach from the previous night had returned with a vengeance. I assumed that this was the father, and I'd really hoped to avoid him. The situation was uncomfortable enough as it was.

The man was probably in his fifties, and had short but unkempt black hair. His jeans and white t-shirt were covered with grease and dirt—he'd probably just gotten off work. There were dark circles under his eyes, and his face had tough, sharp features.

"My name's Jason," I said.

He glared at me. "I've already got a church."

"No, that's not why I'm here. Look, I feel like a complete jackass being here, but there was an incident last night. Some friends and I had too much to drink and I let them talk me into looking inside the shed."

The man sat up. "You peeping at my daughter?" His angry tone concerned me a little, as if he might whip out a pocketknife and slam it into my face.

"No, nothing like that. I mean, sort of like that, but we weren't spying on her or anything. Just a quick glance. I didn't even know anybody was in there."

"Well, now you do. And now you can mind your own goddamn business."

"That's exactly what I plan to do," I said. "I'm only here so I can apologize. I really feel terrible about this. There's no excuse for it."

The man took a drag from his cigarette. "So apologize."

"I'm sorry."

"Good. Now you can go."

I stood there for a moment, feeling awkward. "I was actually here to apologize to your daughter, if that's okay."

"It's not okay."

"She deserves an apology."

"I'll pass on the message."

I sighed. I could hear the sound of Blister's sob, playing over and over in my mind. "Sir, I'm not trying to cause problems for anybody. I just think she deserves to hear 'I'm sorry' from the guy who behaved like a jerk last night, and I'd feel a lot better about myself if I could apologize in person. And I brought something for her."

He looked directly into my eyes, as if trying to discern my true intent. Then he shrugged, crushed the cigarette out onto the armrest of the rocking chair, and stood up. "I'll take you back there. You make it quick, and then I don't want to see you around here again."

"Thank you. Your name is...?"

"Malcolm."

"Thanks, Malcolm."

I felt a queasy sense of dread as we walked back to the shed. Why hadn't I just let him apologize on my behalf? All I'd done was peek in her window; it wasn't like I needed to drop to my knees and grovel for forgiveness. Maybe I should just say, "*Actually, you're right, I shouldn't disturb your daughter any further"* and head back to the cabin.

No. I needed to do the right thing. I'd failed to do the right thing many, many times during my life, but I was an adult and I wasn't going to weasel out of a simple apology.

Malcolm rapped on the shed door. "Rachel! I'm bringing in company! Get decent."

He waited for a moment, then pulled the door open. He walked inside and, after a brief hesitation, I followed him.

The shed smelled nice, as if somebody had been burning cinnamon-scented candles. It really was difficult to even justify calling it a shed from the inside. It was more like a very tiny house, maintained with more love and care than my own place.

Blister—Rachel—sat on her bed. She wore a faded pink nightgown and a light blue plastic mask. It had small slits for the eyes, rosy cheeks, and a too-wide smile. Very unnerving.

"Hi," I said.

She said nothing. I couldn't even be certain that she was looking at me.

I resumed speaking before the silence could become too uncomfortable. "I don't know if you recognize me. I'm the fool who peeked in your window last night."

Rachel gave an almost imperceptible nod. It almost looked like a doll that you're sure you only *imagined* moved its head.

"That was uncool beyond belief. I will never drink again. I just wanted to come by and say that I'm truly sorry, and I hope I didn't ruin your evening."

She remained silent. Her right hand was trembling, and she used it to smooth out her nightgown a bit.

Malcolm stood there, arms folded. "Are you done?"

"Almost." I pointed to the decorations on the wall. "I saw that you like owls. I'm actually an artist, a cartoonist. My work isn't as good as the ones you've already got, but I did this for you."

I unrolled the paper and held up the drawing I'd done of an owl. Though I wasn't that skilled at drawing birds I thought it had turned out pretty well.

She stood up so quickly that I flinched. Just a reflex, but I mentally kicked myself. Great. I was here to apologize, and I was acting like she was some horrific doll-creature coming at me to eat my flesh.

Rachel lowered her head a bit and slowly sat back down on the bed. I walked over to her, forcing myself not to move at a tentative, cautious pace, and handed her the drawing.

She took it from me and held it in front of her mask, looking at it closely. "Thank you," she said, in a soft, scared voice.

"No problem."

She adjusted her mask and spoke even more softly. "I like it." She had a pleasant voice, not the ghastly growl or the high-pitched cackle I would've expected.

Her father cleared his throat and she placed the drawing in her lap.

"Anyway, it's just a way of saying I'm sorry." I shifted a bit, ready to leave. I could feel a trickle of sweat running down the side of my face, but didn't want to call attention to it by wiping it away.

"Thank you."

"You're welcome."

"People aren't...people aren't usually nice to me."

I wasn't sure how to respond to that.

"We're done here, right?" Malcolm asked.

I took a step toward the doorway. "Anyway, sorry once more about last night, and enjoy the owl."

"It's my favorite one. What else do you draw?"

"I do a comic strip. It's called *Off Balance*. There aren't any owls in it. I might add some, now that I've had practice. There aren't that many owls in comic strips, except for that 'Give a Hoot, Don't Pollute' one. That's not a comic strip, though." I realized that I was nervously babbling and shut the hell up.

"I'd like to read it someday."

"Okay."

I had the feeling that if I didn't leave soon, her father really was going to stab me in the face with something, so I quickly stepped out of the cabin. Malcolm followed me, pushing the door closed with more force than was probably necessary.

"You happy now?" he asked.

"Yeah. I just wanted to say I was sorry."

"And now you have."

He walked me to the front of the house, then sat back down on his rocking chair, clearly indicating that I was supposed to leave. I got back in my car and drove away.

Wow. That was one of the weirdest, creepiest encounters of my life, and I'd had some weird, creepy encounters over the years.

I was glad it was over.

Anyway, I'd done the right thing and I felt better about myself after paying that little visit. Assuming that she hadn't already crumpled up the owl picture and asked "Who the hell ever told that untalented hack that he could draw?" I'd made her happy.

Not many people are nice to me...

I didn't really owe her anything beyond my apology—it's not like I'd vandalized her home and contaminated her drinking water. A quick "I'm sorry" and a drawing of an owl and my karmic debt was complete.

Still...

I had copies of all six *Off Balance* collections at the cabin. If she wanted to read them, it couldn't hurt to drop some off. I sure wasn't going to spend any more quality time with her crabby dad, and I had no intention of carrying on another uncomfortable conversation with a chick in a creepy mask, but why not leave a couple of books by her door? I might get a new fan.

I couldn't quite explain why I didn't simply want to erase the incident from my memory. I guess I felt sorry for her. Hard not to feel sorry for a burnt-up girl locked in a shed in the woods. Once I'd burnt my finger on a hot stove and acted like a total baby for the rest of the evening, so I couldn't even imagine the horror of having her entire face burnt—and cut.

Did it still hurt?

So I'd leave her a couple of books. Add an extra bit of reading pleasure to her life. No big deal.

CHAPTER FOUR

V ery early the next morning, Ignatz woke me up by pushing his food dish all over the wooden floor. It was something that dumb dog did on a regular basis, but usually I wasn't sleeping so close to the source of the noise.

"Knock it off," I called out.

Ignatz did not knock it off.

"I'm gonna nail that thing to the floor if you don't quit it," I informed him. "And I mean your nose, not the bowl."

Unfortunately, my dog was both disobedient and didn't understand human English, so I finally just mumbled a few anti-canine curses and got up. I showered, got dressed, microwaved an inedible breakfast burrito, and then signed copies of my first two Off Balance collections, *That Bug Has Issues* and *I Tripped Over My Own Shadow*. (I'd originally called it *Tripping Over Shadows*, but the publisher thought that might have drug connotations. I was fully prepared to fight the sheer stupidity of this until I decided that I liked *I Tripped Over My Own Shadow* better.)

I drove back to Blister's house. If there was a car in the

driveway, I was going to drive right on past, since I had no particular interest in having her dad force-feed me a shotgun. If he wasn't there, I'd drop off the books and speed away. (Which, I had to admit, was very much the sort of immature behavior that got me into this situation to begin with, but I figured that leaving a couple of Off Balance collections at her doorstep wasn't quite the same as, say, leaving a bag of burning dog crap. Some critics would disagree.)

There was no vehicle in her driveway. I pulled in, shut off the engine, and grabbed the plastic bag that contained the books and a short *"Hope you enjoy these!"* note with a smiley face. Inexplicably feeling like a criminal, I quickly walked over to the shed, set the bag of books down in front of the door, and—

"What the hell are you doing?"

I glanced over into the woods. Blister, wearing her plastic mask, stood about twenty feet away. She was wearing blue jeans and a t-shirt. Most noteworthy, she had a revolver pointed at me.

I'd never had a firearm aimed at me before. It was a lot scarier than I would've expected. I immediately raised my hands in the air. "Don't shoot!"

"What do you want?"

"Just dropping off some books. That's all. Really."

"What books?"

"My books. Cartoon books."

She walked toward me, closing the gap between us by half. "Why?"

"I just, y'know, thought you might want to read them. You'd said something about that yesterday, so I figured, well, I've got the books, and I thought I could save you a trip to the bookstore." *Babbling. You're babbling.* "I know it's kind of weird to give books away for free when that's how I make my living, but I got paid for the original strips when they ran in papers, so it's sort of like getting paid for them twice. Well, not sort of, exactly like getting paid for them twice." *Still babbling. Stop it.* "It's good business to give away free samples. I figure, if you enjoy these, you might buy the others. I know, I probably should've knocked on your door and just given them to you, but I'll be honest and say that your dad scares me."

"My dad isn't here."

"I know. The gun scares me, too."

She regarded me for a moment. At least I think she was regarding me—it was hard to tell exactly what she was doing through that mask. "Thanks for the books," she finally said.

"You're welcome."

"You can put your arms down."

I slowly lowered my arms.

There was another long, uncomfortable silence. Finally she spoke again. "Do you want to come inside?"

I didn't, not really, but she was still pointing the revolver at me. "Uh, sure."

"You don't have to."

"No, I'd like to."

She lowered her arm. "Sorry about the gun."

"That's okay. Guns protect people."

"You really don't have to come inside. I was just offering. I've got Cherry Coke."

"I'm always up for Cherry Coke."

She nodded and walked up to her door. I stepped back to get out of her way. I was perspiring in a very unattractive manner but, as before, I didn't want to call attention to it by mopping off my forehead. She opened the door and walked inside. After a moment of hesitation, I followed her.

"I didn't expect you to be outside," I said. It was a lame comment, I knew, but I'd made so many lame comments by this point that they all sort of blurred together.

"My dad lets me walk outside. He doesn't keep me caged up like an animal."

"I'm sorry. That's not what I meant."

"No, it's okay. It *is* a pretty messed-up situation." She pulled the books out of the bag and looked them over. "Thank you. I've never met a cartoonist."

"No problem. I've never met a..." I wasn't quite sure how I'd intended that sentence to conclude, so I let it drift away and hoped she didn't notice. I shifted my weight awkwardly. I wasn't used to being so uncomfortable in social situations—I was typically an outgoing kind of guy—but I felt like a teenager asking for his first date.

"Do you want to sit down?"

I sat down on the couch. Blister—Rachel—walked over to a small portable refrigerator, opened the door, and took out two Cherry Cokes. "Do you want it in a glass with ice, or just the can?" she asked.

"The can's fine."

She nodded and brought me the Cherry Coke. I popped it open and took a long gulp. The silence continued, so I took another long gulp to fill it.

Rachel spoke first. "Can I ask you a question?"

"Sure."

She tapped her plastic chin. "This mask—it's creepy, isn't it?"

I wasn't entirely certain how to respond to that. "Hell yeah!" would be a poor answer if it turned out that she'd made the mask herself. I settled for a non-committal shrug.

"Be honest," she said.

"Yeah, it is, kind of."

"I hate it. It's itchy. I don't care what you look like, how gross your face is, a mask is more unnerving, don't you think?"

"I'd agree with that."

"Maybe if the mouth moved it would be okay, I don't know. For a long time my face was wrapped in gauze. It was actually a better look, but it's too much of a pain to wrap myself up every day." She sighed. "You saw my face already, right?"

"Just a glimpse."

Rachel hesitated. "Do you mind if I get rid of this creepy thing so we can talk like regular human beings?"

"No, no, not at all, go ahead."

I braced myself and put on my best poker face as she slowly removed the mask. I'm pretty sure my expression didn't give anything away, but...dear God...

It wasn't that I couldn't handle the sight of a burn victim. I'd seen burn victims before (though, admittedly, never this close and never this bad). But in addition to the scar tissue, her face looked like it had been assembled from a dozen jagged pieces that didn't quite fit together properly, like a skull that had some burnt flesh haphazardly slapped onto the surface. Her mouth was in better shape, and also the area around her eyes, but the rest was an absolute mess.

I remembered what the bait store cashier had said: she'd been cut as well as burnt. *Savagely* cut, from the looks of it. Scraping bone.

I felt sick to my stomach—not because of her appearance, but at the thought that somebody had done this to her on purpose.

"Do you want me to put it back on?" she asked.

"No." I quickly looked away.

"Thanks. I really hate that thing. If I start looking too disgusting, let me know and I'll turn out the lights."

"No, that's okay," I said, not sure if she was kidding or not. An instant later I decided that she was.

She pulled a chair out from the shed's one table and sat down. "Sorry about the gun."

"No problem."

"You can never be too safe."

"Absolutely."

"And my dad makes me carry it when I go out for a walk."

"That's not surprising." I took another drink. I'd almost emptied the can already. "Does he make you wear the mask whenever you go outside?"

"He makes me carry it around in case I run into somebody. Or, I guess, in case somebody is standing at my door trying to sneak over some books. When I first got back home I tried to class it up with porcelain masks, but I broke about twenty of the stupid things and had to switch to plastic. So now I kind of feel like white trash."

I had to laugh out loud at that. I now felt slightly more relaxed. Sure, my sense of relaxation was still somewhere between "in the dentist's chair for a quartet of root canals" and "what's that creature doing on the wing of the plane?" but I appreciated the mild improvement.

"Do you live around here?" she asked.

I shook my head. "Nope. Just visiting."

"Relatives?"

"I'm staying at my agent's cabin. There was sort of an incident and he wants me to stay out of the public eye for a while."

"What kind of incident?"

"Here, you be the judge. Let's say that that these horrible little kids were throwing rocks at your dog, and you asked them nicely to stop, and then you went to one of their mothers and she didn't care. So the next time they threw rocks, you burst out of your house with a fake severed head and a fake chainsaw, and you were covered with fake blood, and the kids flipped out and ran away, and one of them fell and broke his arm. Is that funny?"

Rachel was silent for a very long moment, her face completely motionless. Finally, she spoke: "That's fucking hilarious."

"I know, right? Thank you! Thank you so much!" I was becoming a huge Blister fan.

"Is the kid going to be okay?"

"Yeah, the little piece of crap will be fine. I broke my arm on the monkey bars once. It's all part of being a kid."

I finished off the Cherry Coke, and then realized that my owl drawing was up on her wall, prominently displayed.

"Glad you liked the owl," I said, gesturing toward it with my empty can.

"I love it."

"So do you ever get to go out and...do stuff?"

"Are you asking me out?"

I was glad I was done with my drink, or I would have choked on it. I barely stifled a cough. "No! I mean, no...I mean, no, I was just curious."

"Relax, I was just kidding."

"Not that I—"

"Chill. No, I don't really go anywhere. I don't get a lot of social invitations these days."

"How long have you been...?"

"A disfigured freak?"

I smiled. "You're very dark, you know that?"

"I know. I try to be sunshiny, but the whole 'grotesque monster' part gets in the way."

"You're not a grotesque monster."

"Would you sleep with my picture by your bedside?" she asked.

"Hey, when I was a kid, I slept with a Frankenstein figure by my pillow," I told her. A couple of seconds later I decided that my comment was in extremely poor taste. "Not that I'm saying you look like Frankenstein. I apologize. I didn't mean that."

"Jason, if you say that I have bad breath or body odor, you'll hurt my feelings. Otherwise, it's cool. I'm not an attractive woman."

"When did it happen?"

"Five years ago. Which version of the story did you hear?"

"Boyfriend...blowtorch..."

Rachel nodded. "Oh, then you heard the true one. That's unusual."

"So did he really...I mean, is this something you want to talk about?"

"I don't mind talking about it. Is this something you actually want to hear?"

I nodded.

She leaned a bit closer. "Before I tell you this story, I have to ask: are you scared of clowns?"

"No."

"They terrify me..."

CHAPTER FIVE

Dad made the cake himself. It didn't turn out right, even using mix from a box, and she's pretty sure it's because he forgot the eggs, but Rachel doesn't mind. It's the best cake she's ever had.

"Eighteen years old," Dad says, looking at her from across the table. "Jesus Christ. I'm doomed."

She laughs and blushes. She takes another bite of cake, being careful not to drop any crumbs on her new green dress.

The doorbell rings. Rachel is simultaneously excited and nervous, because she knows who it is, and she knows what they're planning to do.

Dad smiles and nods. "Go on. Leave your Dad all alone on your birthday."

She gets up from the table and goes over to give him a kiss on the cheek. "I'll be home early."

"Yeah, you will. Seven-thirty."

She laughs.

"Okay, midnight. And I'll still be up, so don't go letting your coach turn into a pumpkin."

"Love you, Dad," she says, scurrying out of the kitchen, through the living room, and over to the front door.

Brandon is there, not quite as dressed up as her, but definitely upgraded from his usual attire. He tells her happy birthday and hands her a wrapped present. Excited, she tears the present open, purposely shredding the wrapping paper as much as possible (she's not into the idea of opening gifts with restraint) then removes the lid of the box.

Inside is a tiny clown figurine.

She sighs. "You creep."

"Like it?"

"Yeah, right."

She playfully punches Brandon in the arm as he laughs and makes scary noises with it.

THEY SKIPPED THE MOVIE, just as they'd planned, and now they're parked in his car, kissing. Brandon grabs her breast and she pushes his hand away.

"What?" he asks.

"It's not a squeeze toy."

"We're gonna have sex and I'm not allowed to touch your boob?"

"Be gentle." She grins. "*Mostly* gentle."

"I can work with that."

"You're lucky you get anything. Fucking clown."

"It was a joke!"

"No, jokes are things that are funny. That was just mean. That's not a birthday present."

"Okay, okay," he says. "I've got your birthday present in my pocket."

"I'm sure you do."

"No, seriously."

He reaches into his pocket and takes out a small jewelry box. Rachel's anger vanishes as he hands it to her.

She opens the box.

Inside is a beautiful silver necklace. The charm is a clown face.

"You asshole."

Brandon howls with laughter.

"Do you really think you're getting laid tonight?" she asks.

"Maybe there's something in my other pocket."

"I don't care. You're in a jerk mood and I want you to take me home."

"Seriously, here's the real present," he tells her, taking out a second jewelry box.

"I don't want it. Not tonight. Give it to me tomorrow."

"It's not your birthday tomorrow."

"Brandon, take me home. We're done for now."

"But you promised." He sounds almost whiny.

Rachel gapes at him. "I *promised*? I didn't promise you anything. We had an unofficial agreement to go all the way that was based on you not being a complete dick. I think giving me two scary clown presents voids the deal."

"They weren't scary clowns. They were just clowns."

"Take me home."

Brandon quickly tries to reach under her dress. She shoves him away.

"What the hell? Did you really just do that? What, are you a rapist now?"

Brandon looks confused and humiliated. "I'm not a rapist," he says, softly.

"Well, you're an idiot and a jerk and an ex-boyfriend. Thanks for ruining my birthday."

"Ex-boyfriend? For real? You can't break up with me over this."

"We'll talk about it tomorrow. For now I just want you to take me home."

"Okay, okay, I'm sorry," he says.

And then he lunges forward and slams her head into the dashboard.

RACHEL OPENS HER EYES. She thinks she's in a cabin. It's too dark to see for sure. She's strapped to a mattress on the floor, and there's a rag shoved in her mouth, packed in so tightly that she can't spit it out.

She lets out a muffled scream and violently struggles, but she can't get free.

There's a *flick* sound, and then, about ten feet away, the flame of a lighter illuminates a scary clown mask.

No, a whole clown suit, complete with oversized red shoes. The clown slowly walks forward, making a deliberate attempt to be frightening, and then crouches down next to her.

The lighter flame goes out.

When the flame returns, Brandon is holding a straight razor.

Rachel screams again.

The clown silently lashes out with the razor, cutting deep.

Rachel continues to scream as the clown slashes again and again.

The lighter goes out.

The clown continues to mutilate her face in total darkness.

The illumination of a flame returns, but this time it's the flame of a blowtorch.

Rachel shrieks until her vocal cords don't work anymore.

CHAPTER SIX

"I'm sorry," said Rachel, apparently noticing my horrified expression. "Did I overshare?"

"What? Oh, no. No, you didn't." I took a non-existent drink of my Cherry Coke.

"That was probably a bit graphic for our second conversation. My social skills have eroded."

"How did you get away?"

"I didn't. He got distracted by something, then quit burning me and left. I eventually got loose. And then it was hospital time. They can do miraculous things these days, apparently, but not so much for me. I guess it wasn't a very good hospital."

"Jesus."

"People call me Blister. I called myself Gauze Girl. The day they unwrapped me for the first time...not my best."

"Brandon's in jail, right?"

Rachel shook her head. "Nobody ever saw him again."

"Are you scared he'll come back?"

"Five years later? Not really. If I were a betting woman, I'd say that he ran out deep into the woods, put a bullet in his own brain, and became a nice meal for the local wildlife."

"Wouldn't bones and stuff have turned up?"

Rachel laughed. "This isn't one of your big-city razor-cutting-and-blowtorch-burnings. They looked for him, but there weren't a lot of forensics involved."

"So he could still be at large," I said. Yeah, I knew that it sounded really corny.

"See, now you sound like my dad," said Rachel. "He won't let me leave. I'm lucky he lets me have this shed to myself. If it were up to him, I'd stay in the house. At least this way I can pretend I've got my own place."

"Would you leave if you could?"

"Maybe. Probably not. I think about it all the time, but I can scare kids even without a fake chainsaw. There aren't a lot of opportunities out there for me."

"There's got to be something better than hiding away like this."

"You think so? Didn't you and your buddies come over here to gape at a monster?"

Ouch. "They weren't my buddies. Hey, do you want to go out on a paddleboat?"

"Excuse me?"

"I've got a paddleboat back at the cabin. We could go out on the lake."

"Oh...no, there's no way."

"Why not?"

"My dad would go berserk."

"But he'd be mostly mad at me, right? I'm willing to take the risk if you are."

"I don't know."

"We'll be sneaky," I insisted. "He'll never find out."

"Sneaky. On a paddleboat. In the middle of a lake."

Clearly, I needed to sweeten the deal. "I've got ice cream bars in the freezer."

WE SAT NEXT to each other on the paddleboat in the middle of the lake. Rachel had agreed to come with me, but not without a mask, so she currently was wearing the likeness of Marilyn Monroe. She slipped the ice cream bar under the mask as we worked the pedals.

"What do you want to talk about that's more cheerful than the details of my disfigurement?" she asked.

"What's your favorite movie?"

"*Scarface.*"

"Are you joking?"

"Yes."

I smiled. "You need to hold up a sign or something."

"It's *Dumbo.*"

"*Dumbo.* Solid choice."

"What's yours?"

"*Fritz the Cat.*"

"I haven't heard of that one."

"It's animated," I said, leaving out the fact that it was X-rated.

"So we both like living in a cartoon world."

"Hey, it's how I make my living. Although I don't so much draw elephants on acid trips."

"He was drunk."

"I've been drunk. Pink elephants on parade are not alcohol based."

"Don't taint my childhood memories," said Rachel. "My mom took me to see *Dumbo* the day before she died."

"Are you joking?"

"No."

"Then I feel like a bastard and withdraw my comment. How did she die?"

"Remember, I started the movie conversation to lighten the tone."

"Right. Favorite song?"

"'Somewhere Over The Rainbow.' Yours?"

"'Timothy.'"

"I don't know that one," Rachel admitted.

"It's about miners trapped in a cave-in who resort to cannibalism. Really catchy tune. The Buoys. 1970."

"So I was eight when it came out. Wasn't listening to a lot of cannibalism-themed music at that time in my life."

"Jeez, you're young."

"How old are you?"

"Thirty-eight."

"Wow," said Rachel. "You could be my dad."

"The hell I could."

"You could if you dropped out of high school with a pregnant girlfriend!"

I glared at her in mock disdain. "How's your goddamn ice cream?"

As I PULLED my car back into her driveway, Rachel removed her Marilyn Monroe mask. I'd been worried that her dad might have come home early, but the driveway was empty.

"Well, thank you for getting me out of the house," she said, extending her hand.

I shook it. "You're welcome. I enjoyed it."

"Yeah, me too."

"Are you going to be around tomorrow?"

"I could try to clear my social calendar."

"Same time?"

"Sure." Rachel opened the door and started to get out of the car, but then stopped and looked back at me. "This isn't just pity, is it?"

"Of course not," I said, and I meant it. I'd thoroughly enjoyed her company today.

"Thanks. I'll see you tomorrow."

She got out of the car and closed the door. As she walked away, I realized that I should have gotten out and opened the door for her. Or would that have made it feel like a date? This wasn't supposed to be a date. This was just friendship.

I watched her walk past her father's house to her shed, which I knew I should quit thinking of as a shed. She turned and waved as I drove away.

When I got back to the cabin, I called Chuck. "What's going on?" I asked as he answered.

"Good news," he said. "They aren't going to sue you, and you're going to buy nice shiny new uniforms for their soccer team."

"How sweet of me. Can I put chainsaw logos on their shirts?"

"Ha," said Chuck, but not in a legitimately amused way. "I don't know how you can do a daily comic strip and have so much wit left over. How's your rage?"

"All gone."

"Good. Then you can come home."

I hadn't expected to be released from my banishment so soon. "I'm actually enjoying this place," I told him. "I think I might hang out here another day or two, if that's okay."

I could almost hear Chuck frown. "Why? What the hell is going on up there?"

"Nothing. Just enjoying the peace and quiet. Making new friends."

"Are you bringing women to my cabin?"

"No."

"Are you having sex in my bed?"

"No."

"You swear?"

"I met this girl, but it's not like that at all."

"I told you not to do anything in my bed. That was my one request. Make yourself at home, help yourself to anything in the cupboards, use my fishing tackle all you want, but don't contaminate my bed."

"I've done nothing in your bed," I promised him.

"Keep it that way."

"It's purely a friendship thing. No chance of romance. It's actually kind of bizarre; her face is totally burnt."

"Blister? You're screwing Blister?"

"I'm not screwing anyone! Jesus, Chuck, keep this up and I'll whack it right into your pillowcase. What do you know about Blister?"

"I've heard that her dad keeps her locked in the freaking basement. What the hell are you getting into up there?"

"If you thought that there was really a girl locked in the basement, why didn't you call the cops?"

"Because I didn't believe it."

"Well, good. You shouldn't. She's very sweet and she and I are just friends."

"You're extending your vacation, the vacation that I forced you to take, for a friend?"

"Yes."

Chuck sighed. I could picture him massaging his temples. "Festering Pus gives me no problems. Have I mentioned that? No problems. Zero."

"Talk to you later, Chuck," I said, hanging up.

There was nothing weird about this, right? We were two friends who enjoyed each other's company. If anything was weird, it was the age difference, but she was twenty-three; it wasn't like she was eighteen and still in high school.

Was I completely at ease with her appearance? No, to be completely honest with myself, I wasn't. Not yet. But I was long past the "recoiling in horror" part, and I most definitely did not give a shit what people like Louie and Erik might think. I liked her, which wasn't something I could say about everyone I met. Why not spend more time around somebody I liked?

I PROPOSED A ROAD TRIP. Rachel agreed under the condition that a) we not actually do anything when we got to our destination, and b) she'd keep the mask on. I told her that we'd have a destination-free road trip; simply drive for an hour or two and see where it took us.

I rolled down the windows and cranked up the music, wishing I owned a convertible. As we sped down the highway (obeying the posted speed limits, for the most part), I found myself hoping that Rachel would take off the light blue mask and enjoy the wind against her face. It blew her hair around, but the sensation just wasn't the same through plastic.

The wind was loud, the music was loud, and Rachel wasn't easy to understand through her mask anyway, so we didn't talk much. I didn't care. It was great that we'd somehow already reached the point where it felt totally fine to take a road trip without talking.

We sung along a little bit, but Rachel didn't know the words to many songs in my collection, and when she asked about the availability of specific artists in my cassette collection, her suggestions baffled me. Finally she flipped through my extensive musical library herself, snickering a lot.

A sign along the road suggested that we take a detour to acquire some delicious fresh Georgia peaches, which sounded like a splendid idea. Rachel agreed, as long as she could wait in the car.

I pulled off at the next exit, and the shop was right there. I parked the non-convertible and shut off the engine. "Sure you don't want to come in?"

"I'm sure."

Was I relieved? I hoped not. I supposed I was on some level, maybe even a conscious one. I think it was more the mask than her real face. If you walk to a fruit stand with a disfigured girl and people stare, you can express moral outrage at their rude behavior. If you walk into a shop with a chick in a creepy plastic mask...well, you couldn't really blame them. I'd be staring, too.

"Any requests? I'm not sure what they'll have."

"String cheese."

"Anything else?"

"If they've got cheese with bits of habanero peppers in it, I'd like some of that."

"Wow. I didn't know you were such a wild woman."

"Lots you don't know."

"Do you want a beef stick?" I asked. "Places like this usually have beef sticks."

"Is that innuendo?"

"Oh, yeah. When I ask the ladies if they want me to buy them a beef stick from a fruit shop, they're all over me."

"Well, naturally."

"Seduction tip #271."

"Noted."

"Seriously, though, do you want a beef stick if they have them?"

"No, thank you."

The fruit shop did indeed have beef sticks, though sadly no

string cheese. Rachel pushed her mask forward so that she could eat her peach, but didn't take it off.

They were excellent peaches, despite it not being peach season, so we decided that this was an excellent halfway point for our trip, and headed back.

Now THERE WAS an important issue to bring up. I'd been avoiding it all day, but I couldn't *not* ask her about it. It might be awkward and uncomfortable for both of us, but I felt it was something that we needed to discuss before our relationship went any further.

"Did you read my books?" I asked.

"I can't start a new book until I finish the one I'm reading. I'd have a nervous breakdown. It's an OCD thing, I guess. So I only got to read about twenty pages of the first one."

"And...?"

"It was really cute."

Cute. The pat on the head of artistic feedback. The little kid helping to set the dinner table and forgetting the forks but, hey, it's adorable that he tried.

"Cute, huh?"

"Very cute. I wasn't going to say anything until I'd finished both of them."

"Did you laugh?"

"Sure."

"Out loud?"

Rachel smiled. "Jason Tray, are you *needy*?"

"No, I just wanted to hear what you thought."

"Are you sure? Because I'm detecting a bit of a needy vibe from you."

"I'm always open to honest feedback."

"I'd never pegged you for the needy type," she teased. "If I'd known this about you, I would've said something much sooner. How difficult this day must have been for you."

"Ha ha."

I sure as hell wasn't going to admit this to Rachel, but, yes, when it comes to my work, I'm needy. I'm not saying that I would've stopped talking to her if she'd said, "Wow, that was worse than a 12th century attempt at a colonoscopy." I simply value the opinion of people I care about. I'm allowed to be insecure in this one area, right?

"I'm sorry," said Rachel. "I shouldn't be making fun of you. That's really rude. I think that Zep the Beetle is adorable. I smiled the entire time I was reading."

"See, that wasn't so hard, was it?"

"I THINK I'm going to talk to your dad," I told her, as I pulled into her driveway.

"No!"

"There is nothing whatsoever wrong with us hanging out. Sneaking around like criminals is ridiculous. We're just friends. Even if we weren't, it's not like we're a couple of teenagers."

"Aren't you leaving soon anyway?"

"That's not the point. If two people want to go fishing and eat cheese, they should be allowed to do it."

"Dad loves guns."

I hesitated for a moment, but only a moment. "I'm cool with that."

"I mean, he *really* loves guns. He names them. He sings to them."

"Look, if you really don't want me to talk to him, I won't, but I think it's more respectful for everybody if I do."

"He'll forbid you to ever see me again."

"No, he won't. Well, he *will*, but I'll talk him out of it. I choose my own friends. Anyway, I'm enjoying this place. I'll come back soon. So is it okay if I talk to him?"

Rachel didn't respond right away, and it was hard to tell which way she was leaning. Finally, she nodded. "I'd like that."

"Great. But I won't be here when he gets home. We'll let him unwind and have a drink first."

"Good idea."

Malcolm was seated out on his porch, having a beer, when I returned. He did not look happy to see me. I parked the car, worked up my nerve, then got out and waved.

"Hi, Malcolm," I said.

"I can think of no possible reason that I want to see you here," he said.

I walked up to the porch. "I apologize again for intruding. And I apologize in advance if you don't like what I'm about to say, but—"

"Rachel told me everything."

"Oh."

"So, Jason, I apologize if *you* don't like what *I'm* about to say. If your motives aren't honorable, they'll never find the body."

"That sounds perfectly reasonable."

"Just think of me as an overprotective father times a thousand."

"Yes, sir."

"She likes you," Malcolm informed me. He chuckled. "She'd probably have the hots for you, but you're too old."

"Ah," I said, not having an adequate response. I felt a bit hurt and disappointed, which was kind of stupid, especially since Malcolm was joking. Or at least I thought he was. It was difficult to tell with their family.

Malcolm shifted in his rocking chair. "You like Yahtzee?"

WE SAT on Malcolm's living room floor around the coffee table. It was a sparsely furnished place that could use a good cleaning, but at least I didn't feel like I was going to get any diseases by kneeling here.

Rachel rolled the dice. "Fuck!"

"You watch your mouth," Malcolm told her.

"I've already got my twos! This is bullshit!"

"Don't think that just because you've got a guest, I'm going to let you get away with that kind of language," Malcolm said, though he was kind of laughing as he said it.

I rolled the dice. I'd rolled a small straight on the first try, but I already had both my small and large straights. "Fiddlesticks!"

We played seven games. At first I thought Rachel and Malcolm just really, really enjoyed playing Yahtzee, but the wins were evenly distributed between Rachel and I until the last game, which Malcolm won. Then he said that he was tired and done for the night, and I understood that he couldn't quit until he had a victory.

As Malcolm lay asleep on the couch, Rachel and I watched a riveting half-hour infomercial on television. I'm not being sarcastic. I'm not saying that either us believed that it was quality entertainment, but the audience's nearly orgasmic enthusiasm for this amazing breakthrough in frying pan technology was legitimately riveting to view.

When it ended, I checked my watch. 1:00 AM. "I should go," I said.

"Thank you for another good day."

"Thank *you*. I'll stop by tomorrow."

I drove back to the cabin feeling good. This had been a genuinely enjoyable day. I was glad that Chuck had banished me from polite society for a while. When I returned to Florida, I'd be more relaxed and perhaps less inclined to frighten the neighborhood kids.

I felt somewhat less relaxed upon seeing that Chuck's cabin was engulfed in flames.

CHAPTER SEVEN

Not much later, the cabin was completely wiped out. A couple of firemen sprayed water on the smoldering remains, while I spent quality time with Sheriff Baker. He was in his mid-thirties, slightly overweight, and though he conducted himself in an entirely professional manner I got the sense that this was a fun change in his routine.

Upon seeing the inferno, I'd been in an absolute panic for a couple of minutes, but then Ignatz came running up to me, barking away, and I was able to downgrade to a moderate panic.

"You a smoker?" Sheriff Baker asked.

"No."

Baker wrote that down. "Do you recall leaving the stove on?"

"I didn't use it all day."

"Could be faulty wiring. Could be rats."

"Rats?"

"You know. Rats chewing on the wiring."

"Oh."

Sheriff Baker shrugged. "Probably just one of those things. Your agent, Chuck, I've drank with him a few times, he's a smart guy. He knows the importance of insurance."

"Yeah, he's covered."

"He's not gonna be happy, though."

"No," I said. "I don't think he will be. Are we done? I should probably get that call over with."

"Oh, go right ahead. I wouldn't want to interrupt that. I'm sure I'll have more questions, and I'll probably need you to come down to the station and give me an official statement tomorrow. You'll be around, right?"

"Yeah," I said. I took out my wallet and gave him a business card. "Here."

Sheriff Baker chuckled as he looked at the card. "Zep the Beetle. I love that guy."

"Thanks."

"Maybe you can do a strip where Zep's house burns down."

"Gotta take inspiration where you can get it."

I realized Malcolm was coming toward me. He looked about as unhappy as it was physically possible for a human being to look. Oh, yeah. This was going to be an ugly conversation.

Malcolm walked right up to me, getting in my face. "You stay away from my daughter."

I gestured to the cabin rubble. "Why? Because of this? I have no idea how it happened."

"Well, I do."

"So what are you saying? It was arson?"

"I'm saying for you to stay away from her."

Malcolm turned and began to leave.

"Hey, whoa, whoa, whoa! If you think people are burning down cabins over this, I need more information!" I didn't say this loud enough for Baker or the firemen to hear, but I was sure that

Malcolm heard. He hesitated for a split second, then ignored me and continued walking.

I hurried after him and grabbed his shoulder. Malcolm spun around, looking just a tad homicidal.

"Don't touch me."

"Who do you think it was?" I asked. "Her boyfriend?"

"Don't be stupid."

"How does that make me stupid? You're worried about him coming back, right?"

"No, I am not worried about some maniac coming back for vengeance. It's not about that. I love my daughter, and I like you, but the shitty reality is that some people in this town don't approve of the kind of thing you're doing."

"I'm not doing anything!"

"If they're coming after you, they could come after her next. I won't have Rachel's life put in danger. Stay away."

"Hey, if you know who did this, you need to tell the sheriff."

"I don't know who did it."

Malcolm walked away. I let him go.

As much as I wanted to check on Rachel, I knew that it was a bad idea. I felt like I could smooth things over with Malcolm once he calmed down, but if I went straight back to see his daughter against his will, he'd kick my ass, call the cops to get me arrested for trespassing, and I'd never be welcome there again. Rachel could take care of herself even without her overprotective dad keeping watch. She'd be fine.

I found a motel that allowed dogs. From the condition of the carpet and wallpaper, it also allowed Tasmanian devils. Ignatz went from stain to stain, sniffing away, but at least the room wasn't on fire. Tomorrow I'd have to buy new clothes and other essentials.

I called Chuck. He did not like to be disturbed after 10:00 PM, and he also probably did not like to be disturbed to be told that his cabin had burned to the ground, so this was going to be a highly unpleasant call. I'd rather have waited until tomorrow, but I didn't want him to hear about it from somebody else.

"Chuck? Hi. Jason."

Chuck asked me if I knew what time it was. I assured him that, yes, I did. I apologized for waking him. He accepted my apology and asked what was wrong.

"Um," I said, "remember that whole thing with the kid and the broken arm?"

"Yes."

"I may have trumped it."

"You son of a bitch! What did you do? Did you kill somebody this time? Goddamn it, Jason, do I need to chain you to the wall to keep you out of trouble? What did you do? What Jason Tray mess do I need to clean up now?"

"Is Sarah with you?"

"Of course Sarah's with me! She's my wife and it's two in the morning! What the hell do you think?"

"You know what, put Sarah on, and I'll tell her and let her tell you."

"Tell me what you did, Jason."

"I didn't do anything. But your cabin burned down."

"Excuse me?"

"It's a long story, but that's the basic gist of it," I said. "You can go back to sleep now."

"Was anybody hurt?"

"No."

"Is your dog okay?"

"Yes."

"Did they at least get the pinball machine out?"

"No."

"You son of a bitch! I'm driving over there tomorrow. We'll have lunch. Worst lunch you've ever had."

I was tempted to make a joke about making sure we ate in a public place with plenty of witnesses, but, no, Chuck was not in a humor appreciation mood. "All right."

"Goodnight, Jason."

"Goodnight, Chuck."

CHUCK and I sat across from each other in a booth in a very small restaurant. I poked occasionally at my salad while Chuck silently wolfed down his monster hamburger. The tension was thicker than the grease. This was going to be a "*keep quiet, keep your head down, and let Chuck chew you out until he can chew no more*" situation. It wasn't as if I knocked over a candle or I'd been juggling flaming torches or something, but I wouldn't be making any excuses. The only thing he would get from me was an apology.

"I'm—"

"Don't talk to me yet," Chuck told me through a mouthful of burger.

"I just—"

"Silence!"

I was silent. Chuck finished his burger, wiped his mouth with a napkin, then leaned across the table toward me.

"You are the worst human being who has ever lived," Chuck informed me.

"I'm sorry."

"You know Hitler? I like Hitler more than I like you, and I'm a Jew."

"I think you're being melodramatic."

"I sent you up here to keep you out of trouble. If I'd known that you were going to burn down my cabin I would have set you loose on a little kid arm-breaking rampage instead."

"I don't know what to tell you, except that I'm truly sorry. I have no idea how it happened."

"I know exactly how it happened. I let a dumb-ass stay there."

"It could've been worse," I said.

"Everything could be worse. Hitler could have killed seven million Jews instead of six."

"That's really in poor taste."

"You know those licensing agreements you turned down, like the one for that shitty tasting mint-flavored cereal? We're going to re-evaluate."

"Okay, fine. Whatever it takes to get you to call off the gypsy curse, or the hit men, or whatever horrible pox you've placed upon me."

Chuck glared at me. "Oh, when I place a pox on you, you'll know it. When are you going home?"

"I thought I might stay here a while longer."

"Why would you stay here? To rebuild my cabin?"

"It's not right what he's doing to that girl. You don't keep somebody hidden away like that."

"It's none of your business. Call Social Services if you're so concerned."

"She's twenty-three."

"Exactly. She's an adult. She doesn't need you going on some noble quest to rescue her."

I didn't respond to that.

"Answer me this," Chuck said. "Are you doing this because you care about her, or because you're a stubborn son of a bitch?"

"Both."

"Well, you're going to do whatever you want, regardless of any advice that a smart person gives you, so just be careful."

"I will."

I hesitated for a moment, not sure if I should share my theory with him. But I needed to share it with *someone*.

"I think there was vigilante justice."

"What?"

"I don't think the boyfriend got away. I think they caught him."

"What makes you say that?"

"A feeling, talking to her father. And he made a comment about not being worried that the boyfriend would return for revenge."

"Good Scooby Doo work. Go the hell home."

"I'm staying here."

Chuck sighed. "Well, I'm not your father. Thank God. Try not to burn down your motel."

"I'll do my best."

Since it was Saturday, Malcolm probably wouldn't be at work. It still felt too soon to show up on his property, so I decided to do a bit of investigative work. As a kid, I'd wanted to be a spy, and though that choice was based on fast cars, neat gadgets, and getting to kill hundreds of bad guys, I could relive the fantasies of my youth in a tiny way by chatting with the guy at the bait shop.

I walked into the shop. The same white-bearded cashier from before was behind the counter. My career as an amateur sleuth was off to a good start.

"Well, hello," he said, greeting me with a smile. "Talk around town is that you've been mingling with our local legend."

I strode right over to the counter, attempting to look no-nonsense and perhaps even a bit menacing.

"I know what happened that night," I told him. "I know that you helped murder Brandon Keaton."

We stared at each other for a long moment.

"That's just a wild guess, right?" he asked.

"Yeah," I said, caught. "I figured, what's it gonna hurt?"

The cashier nodded. "What do you know about it?"

"Almost nothing."

"Of course not. We handle our own business here."

"I'm sure you do. I'll give you a hundred dollars to tell me what happened."

"I wasn't there."

"But you know what they did, right?"

"There are a few versions of the story."

"Which one do you believe?"

The cashier didn't respond. I took out my wallet and removed five twenty-dollar bills. I set them on the counter. The cashier looked at them, somewhat longingly, then pushed them back to me.

"Bad form to take bribes," he said.

"Your conscience will heal."

"Can't do it. I won't stop you from buying a hundred dollars' worth of bait, though."

"I really don't want a hundred dollars' worth of worms."

"You could share them with friends."

"Let's pretend that I bought the worms and then reverse-shoplifted them back into the cooler."

The cashier nodded and scooped up the cash. He folded the bills, shoved them into his pocket, then cleared his throat.

"They caught Brandon Keaton the same night," he said. "He didn't go to jail."

"Who caught him?"

"People invested in making sure he didn't get away with it. That's all I can tell you."

"That's all I need."

CHAPTER EIGHT

I started to walk up onto Malcolm's porch, then hesitated. This most definitely fell into the category of "butting into somebody else's business." I didn't have a problem with doing that, but before I confronted Malcolm, I decided that I should talk to Rachel. If *she* wanted me to leave the family alone, I'd leave them alone.

I walked over to the shed and noticed that there was a great big shiny brass fucking padlock on the door. Malcolm had locked his own daughter in the shed. What kind of messed up crap was that? She was his daughter, but was this even legal? Wasn't it technically kidnapping?

Very gently, I knocked on the door.

"Yes?" Rachel asked.

"It's me."

"Hi, Jason."

"Did you know that you're locked in there?"

"Yeah."

"Do you want me to go get a pair of bolt cutters?"

"He's trying to keep me safe."

"You don't keep people safe by locking them away. Did he tell you that somebody burned my agent's cabin down?"

"Yes."

"If anything, he's putting you in danger. If they tried to do the same thing to your place, you'd be trapped in here. You wouldn't be able to get out."

"Dad's watching. I'm sure he's watching you right now."

It occurred to me that, yes, the back of my head was probably visible in a riflescope right now. This realization did not give me a cheerful feeling. I took a deep breath. As long as I didn't start trying to break windows or kick the door down, Malcolm most likely would not fire a bullet into my skull.

"This isn't right," I said. "It's kidnapping. I could have the sheriff come over right now and force him to let you out."

"Please don't."

"Rachel..."

"I shouldn't have gone out. It's my fault."

"That's ridiculous. You can't possibly believe that."

Rachel didn't answer.

"Look," I said, "if you really want me to let this drop, I'll drive back home and you never have to see me again. Is that what you want?"

"Stop being a drama queen."

"I think this is worthy of a little drama."

"You're talking like we're star-crossed lovers."

"I can't help but feel that maybe you aren't understanding that *your father has locked you in there*. There's a padlock on the door. It's a weird, freaky situation. I know you're not a world traveler, but surely you've got to realize that when a dad locks his daughter in her tiny little house, it's not how things usually work."

"I'm not normal. You saw me, right?"

"You were the victim of an awful crime."

"What do you want me to do? Go out and get a job as a fashion model?"

"There's a pretty big middle ground between 'hidden from society' and 'fashion model.'"

"I guess so."

"I'd rather not be friends through a door. If you're done hanging out with me, that's your choice and I'll respect it. But what I'd like you to do is say, 'No, Jason, I enjoy your company. Please go tell my dad what an insane idea this is.'"

"He won't care what you say."

"I think I can persuade him. I don't want to rush you into a decision, but I'm also starting to get worried about his trigger finger. I should probably wrap this up."

She didn't answer.

"Rachel?"

Nothing.

"You still there?"

"Yes, I'm still here," she finally said. I couldn't actually hear her sigh through the door, but the silence felt like it contained a sigh. "Okay. Talk to him if you want. It won't work, but if it'll make you feel better, that's fine."

"Thank you," I said. "I apologize from distracting you from reading my books."

"They're really funny."

I walked up onto Malcolm's front porch and knocked on the door. When he answered, he didn't look at all surprised to see me, and I assumed he'd been watching me through a window, but he still said, "Are you kidding me?"

"I think we should talk."

"Leave my family alone."

"I know what you did to Brandon Keaton. I'm not judging you for it—I would've been right there cheering you on."

"Go away or I'm calling the sheriff."

"You won't call anybody. I'm staying here until you talk to me."

Malcolm slammed the door. I sat down on his rocking chair, prepared to wait him out and call his bluff.

Ten minutes later, the sheriff's car pulled into the driveway. Damn. I stood up as Sheriff Baker got out of the car.

"Don't you have a cabin to rebuild?" he asked me.

"I just want to talk to him."

Sheriff Baker walked onto the front porch. "Now, you know I can't have this kind of thing going on in my town. You're trespassing, and I need you to leave."

"He's got Rachel locked in the shed."

"A man has a right to protect his daughter."

"Protect his daughter by locking her up? That's sick."

"Well, I'll note your objection."

"Sir, I'm not a superstar mega-celebrity, but I have an audience. I have media contacts."

Baker stiffened. "I hope to God that I didn't just hear an attempt to blackmail me."

"No. You heard an extremely formal invitation to chat. Look, I'm not trying to create problems or dig up prior events, but there's a very sweet girl named Rachel who's going through life as a freak named Blister, and it's not fair. I'm just trying to be her friend."

"Some people think you're writing a book."

I shook my head. "I only write four-panel stories. Ten on Sunday. I want to be her friend. That's all."

Without taking his eyes off me, Baker knocked on the door. "Malcolm! Open up."

The door opened. Malcolm glared at me. "Why is he still on my property?" Malcolm asked Baker.

"He wants to talk."

"So?"

"So maybe it's a conversation you should have."

"This is my house. I'll decide who I talk to. I'm not gonna be pushed around by some punk who draws cartoons for a living. How about I break your fingers? How'll you draw funny pictures with both of your hands in a cast?"

"Come on, Malcolm," said Baker. "Don't threaten him with physical violence while I'm standing right here."

"Then do your job and remove him from my front porch."

"I'll leave," I said, "but I'll find out the truth someplace else. I've got resources and lots of free time. Let me say this again: I'm on *your* side. Hell, I'm Rachel's only friend! I'm not looking to have the FBI tear this town apart to find out what really happened to Brandon. I don't want justice for that piece of shit if he's dead. I just need to know what happened."

"Why?" asked Malcolm.

"Because somebody, apparently, is mad at me. I want to be sure it's not him. And though I could wash my hands of the whole situation and just go home, I'm more likely to be a yappy little dog that keeps snarling and biting your feet, no matter how many times you kick him away."

Malcolm scratched the back of his head, looking utterly exasperated. "Why can't you just let this go?

"You killed Brandon, right?" I said.

"Are you going to let him accuse me of murder?" Malcolm asked Baker.

"I swear to God I'm not here to cause problems for you or anybody else involved," I said. "Just tell me what happened."

"He already knows, more or less," said Baker. "Best to go ahead and tell him."

"Are you out of your damn mind?"

"He's right. We don't want journalists and feds swarming around here. This could bite us in the ass, but I'd rather take that risk and trust him at his word than have him blab to the rest of the world that there's some big, dark secret at Lake Gladys."

"You're a lot more trusting than I am," said Malcolm.

"I just know when I'm backed into a corner."

Malcolm closed his eyes and massaged his temples with his thumbs. I was doing a remarkable job of irritating people lately.

"Come on inside," he said.

We went in. Sheriff Baker and I sat down on the couch while Malcolm plopped down on the recliner. He did not offer us any cookies or tea.

"You burn me on this, I'm burning you back," said Malcolm.

Baker shifted uncomfortably. "Again, I wish you wouldn't threaten him while I'm sitting right here."

"Fine," said Malcolm. "After Rachel told us what happened, we tracked down that piece of garbage Brandon Keaton. Caught him before he fled town. I broke his jaw with a baseball bat and told him that if we ever saw him again, I'd kill him. We never saw him again."

I stared at Malcolm for a moment. "That's it?"

"That's it."

"Bullshit."

"Are you calling me a...okay, yeah, it's bullshit." Malcolm sighed. "If you're that damn nosy, I guess I've got no choice but to tell you how it went down."

CHAPTER NINE

Brandon is easy to find. There's a park about a block from his house, and as they drive by, Norman points out the window of the pickup truck. "Hey, is that him?"

Malcolm slows down. "I think so. Yep. I'll be damned."

The kid is sitting there on a swing. Malcolm thought they were going to have to pound on his front door and force his parents to give him up, or drive around Gladys Lake all night searching for him, but he's right there.

Malcolm pulls the truck into a parking spot. Brandon looks in their direction but makes no effort to run. He just sits there.

"You guys stay here," Malcolm says to Norman and Gene. "Be ready to chase him if he tries to run for it."

"Sure we shouldn't call the police?" asks Gene.

"That a joke?"

"I'm just saying, you're pretty upset."

"Shouldn't I be?"

"Hey, if it were my daughter, I'd run the son of a bitch over with my car. So I'd want guys like you and Norman here to talk some sense into me before I did something I might regret."

"I don't want anyone to talk sense into me," says Malcolm. "You knew what we were doing here."

"I didn't think you actually *meant* it."

"You out?"

Gene looks over at Brandon, who is still sitting on the swing. "Norman can stay here and make sure the little monster doesn't go anywhere before the cops get here. I'll come with you back to the hospital. Rachel needs you."

"Rachel's not coming out of surgery for hours. I can sit there helplessly in a waiting room and try to send goddamn brain waves of support through the wall to her, or I can make sure there's justice. You out?"

"I don't know."

"You out?"

"Don't pussy out on us, Gene," says Norman. "The kid wrecked Rachel's face. What kind of life is that girl going to have? She may not even make it through the night."

"Hey, fuck you," said Malcolm.

"It's true, right?"

"No, it's not true! She's not gonna die! They're fixing her up! But while we're sitting here with our thumbs up our butts talking about it, he could decide to run. Gene, if you don't want to help us give that little shit what he deserves, that's fine. You can walk home. But I'm sure as hell not going to wait around to let the system take care of this. Fuckin' jury of his peers might send him home to his mommy and daddy to play Atari. Ain't happening."

Gene scratches his arm as if a few ants are suddenly crawling over it. "All right, yeah, that was crappy of me. We're talking about your daughter. Brandon doesn't deserve three square meals a day in jail. Screw that."

"Thank you," says Malcolm. "I owe you guys big-time, and I won't forget it."

He opens the truck door and gets out. Brandon watches carefully as Malcolm reaches into the back of the truck and picks up a shovel. Malcolm is ready for the kid to bolt, but he doesn't, he just sits there, not even swinging, as Malcolm walks over to him.

Brandon's been crying. Oh boo hoo hoo.

"You know why I'm here, right?" Malcolm asks.

"Yeah."

"Why didn't you run?"

Brandon shrugs. "I know what I've got coming to me. Not gonna hide."

"I respect that."

"How's Rachel doing?"

"How the fuck do you think she's doing? You don't get to ask that. You don't get to pretend you care about her."

"I still do."

Malcolm wants to split his head open with the shovel blade right now. "Don't sit there on a swing like a three-year-old. Stand up. Talk to me like a man."

Brandon stands up. "Did you call the sheriff?"

"He's been notified."

"Is he on his way?"

"I hope not."

Brandon frowns. He looks at the shovel in Malcolm's hand as if seeing it for the first time. "Mr. Kramer, I did something terrible, and I'm going to accept my punishment, but you need to take me to the sheriff's department."

"The hell I do."

"You just going to kill me right here?"

"Thinking about it."

"You can't do that."

"You hurt my little girl."

"I know I did. I hurt her, and I can never take it back, and I'm sorry as hell."

Brandon is definitely going to make a run for it. Malcolm doesn't look away from him, but he gestures with his free hand. The truck door opens.

"Help!" Brandon shouts. "Help me, somebody!"

Malcolm smacks the shovel blade against the side of his head, and the kid drops to the ground. He shuts up for a couple of seconds, then clutches at the bleeding wound and groans in pain.

"Oh my God," says Gene, as he and Norman hurry over to the swing set. "I didn't think you'd really do it."

"We need to get out of here," says Norman, kneeling down and stuffing a towel into Brandon's mouth, before putting a cloth sack over his head. "I can't believe somebody hasn't driven by already."

The plan was to tie him up and throw him in the back of the truck. Gene's got the rope in his hand, but that'll take too long. There's not much traffic in this area, but Norman is right, they can't linger in the middle of a park.

If he's not tied up, he'll jump out of the truck.

Unless his legs don't work.

Malcolm bashes the shovel against Brandon's left knee. The kid's muffled scream might be loud enough to draw attention if there happens to be a pedestrian walking nearby, but none of the neighbors will hear it from their homes. Then he shatters Brandon's right knee.

"Take this," he says, handing the shovel to Gene. To Norman, he says, "You take his arms. I'll take his legs." Malcolm wants to take his broken legs because he doesn't plan to be gentle when they carry him to the truck.

They pick him up. Brandon struggles but is easy to manage. They toss him into the back of the truck and then get back inside.

Malcolm had been meaning to get a new muffler. He's glad now that he didn't. The sound of his noisy-ass truck will cover Brandon's muted efforts to call for help.

They don't drive long.

Then they carry him deep into the woods.

Malcolm plans to make it last. But when Norman yanks off the sack and Malcolm gazes at this pathetic, sobbing piece of crap, he decides that he just wants this over with.

He hoists the shovel over his head like a mallet at a test-your-strength game, and brings it down upon Brandon's face.

It's very obvious to all three of the men that this hit did what it was supposed to do.

Malcolm hits him again, just to be sure.

He uses that same shovel to dig a hole.

They bury the body.

Then they walk back to the truck, not speaking. They don't speak during the entire drive to the hospital.

THERE IS A WITNESS. A guy is out for an evening stroll, listening to music on his Walkman, when he sees three men bash somebody's legs with a shovel, throw him into the back of their truck, and drive away.

He hurries home and calls the sheriff's department, identifying the man with the shovel as Malcolm Kramer.

When news breaks about the horrific attack on Rachel Kramer, whose assailant has gone missing, the witness calls Sheriff Baker to say that he must have been mistaken, he'd seen nothing at the park, sorry for the inconvenience.

"What the hell is the matter with you?" Sheriff Baker asks.

"Nothing at all," Malcolm tells him.

"I know you're responsible for Brandon Keaton's disappearance. Why didn't you let me handle it?"

"You gonna arrest me?"

"I'll probably have to! Seriously, Malcolm, why would you do this? Your daughter will need you more than she's ever needed you before, and you could end up in prison. What would Gabby say?"

"Leave Gabby out of this."

"No, I will not, God rest her soul. You think she's looking down at you and approving of what she sees? You swore to that woman on her deathbed that you'd take care of your daughter. You *swore* it. I was there. You think you did what's best for Rachel right now? Is that what you think? Because from my perspective, rotting away in a prison cell isn't exactly taking care of her."

"He tried to rape her. Then he cut up her face. Then he burned her. Do you think I'm taking care of Rachel by letting him go free?"

"He wouldn't *have* gone free, you moron. You said he wasn't even trying to deny it! Goddammit, Malcolm, I can't believe how badly you screwed up. And you're bringing two fine men down with you. Norman and Gene have to live with that now. That kind of shit haunts you forever."

"I don't know what you want me to say."

"I don't want you to say anything. I don't want to hear your idiot voice." Sheriff Baker rubs his eyes. They sit in silence for a full minute. "A boy gets rebuked, and his balls are so blue that he just snaps. Hell, maybe he would've done it anyway; we'll never know. What happened isn't in dispute. If I was Brandon Keaton, and I'd done this, and I knew I wasn't going to get away with it, I might just run away. If he's never seen again, well, the lucky bastard might have made it to Mexico."

"Yeah," says Malcolm. "He sure might have."

"So what might save your dumb ass is that it makes perfect sense for him to disappear, even if his skull wasn't caved in with a shovel. Folks around here will demand that we look for him to bring him to justice, but they won't be demanding that we search the woods for a shallow grave."

"And they shouldn't."

"No, they *should*, because you're a murderer. Don't start thinking that I'm conceding moral ground here. And don't start breathing any sighs of relief, because that boy has a mother and a father, and *they* might start demanding that we look for shallow graves."

Malcolm nods. "But I'm not under arrest?"

"Not right now."

BRANDON'S PARENTS visit Rachel every day in intensive care. They help pay for her medical bills. They cry a lot. They plead for forgiveness.

They do not ask the police to search for their son.

CHAPTER TEN

W hen somebody has just confessed to beating somebody else to death with a shovel, and the sheriff is sitting right there, it's best to choose your words carefully.

"Thank you for telling me," I said, since that seemed like a good start.

"So where does this leave us?" Malcolm asked.

I wasn't entirely sure. It wasn't as if I wanted to jump to my feet and offer a high five for what he'd done to Brandon. But I couldn't help but think, *Good. Fuck that guy. He got what he deserved.*

I'd like to think that if I'd been in the park with them on that fateful night, I would've put forth a passionate defense against murdering Brandon. I can't say with complete honesty that I would've gone as far as trying to wrestle the shovel out of Malcolm's hands, but I'm almost positive that I would've used the mighty power of speech to make it clear that this was perhaps not the best way to handle this particular situation.

With Brandon dead and buried for five years...I don't know. I was kind of glad they did it. I'm not sure what that says about me as a human being. You're not supposed to approve of bashing an eighteen-year-old boy in the skull with a shovel, regardless of what crime he committed.

I was most definitely not ready to shout, "*The truth must be told! The world must know the facts behind the disappearance of Brandon Keaton!*"

Nope. I wasn't going to say a damn thing.

"Your secret is one hundred percent safe with me," I said. "I needed to know what happened, and now I do, so as far as I'm concerned, we don't need to bring it up again."

Malcolm narrowed his eyes, as if he didn't believe me.

"I'm serious," I assured him. "Even if I thought you were completely in the wrong, I wouldn't say anything. I'd never put Rachel through that."

Now Malcolm was staring at me as if trying to unlock psychic abilities. Then he glanced over at Sheriff Baker, looked back at me, and seemed to relax. "Well, thank you," he said. "I appreciate that."

He stood up and held out his hand. I stood up and shook it. Yes, we'd just shaken hands on me not telling anybody about that one time he murdered an eighteen-year-old boy. This was an odd vacation.

"Rachel doesn't know about this, right? That's what I've been assuming, but I guess I could be wrong."

"No. She does not. As far as she knows, her boyfriend ran away and never came back."

"I'll never tell her," I said.

This now meant, of course, that only a couple days into our friendship, I had a monstrous secret. I'm not actually good with secrets, having accidentally blabbed about no fewer than four surprise parties in the past. I wasn't too worried, though. I figured I could carry on a conversation with Rachel without blurting out, *"By the way, your dad murdered your psycho ex-boyfriend!"*

"There's no reason for her to know," said Sheriff Baker, even though I thought we'd already established that. "It won't do anybody any good."

"I agree." I considered making the zipping-my-lips gesture, but decided it was too cutesy given the context. "But now that we've established that I'm cool with vigilante justice, we still have to talk about Rachel."

"What about her?" Malcolm asked.

"You know what I mean."

"I won't have people making fun of my daughter, and I won't put her in danger. She doesn't need to be walking around town, having people whisper about her. It's not right. If you were a father, you'd understand how I feel."

"I don't think I would."

"Your cabin went up in flames after you started associating with Rachel. Now, maybe somebody was trying to send a message, and maybe you just weren't careful with a space heater, but either way, my daughter might be in danger."

"Might," I said. "Might be."

"Might's enough."

"If it is somebody who doesn't approve of your daughter having a social life, why let them win? Why on earth would you let them push you and Rachel around like that? You fucked up the last guy who messed with her. You shouldn't hide her away like a—and I apologize for my word choice—freak. She's not a freak. She's a great person. Let her try to have a normal life."

"She doesn't want one."

"That can't be true."

"And how long have you known her? What exactly makes you an expert on what my daughter wants?"

"I'm a friend. I'm not trying to criticize your parenting skills, but I think I can read people well enough to decide if they're the type of person who wants to be locked in a shed for the rest of their life. For some kids, give them a video game system and they're fine. I don't put Rachel into that category. This isn't right, Malcolm."

"I'm never one to pry into family matters," said Sheriff Baker, "but I do have to admit, locking her in there is a trifle extreme."

"I didn't ask for your opinion," said Malcolm.

"Well, you didn't ask for his opinion, either, and I figured that if unsolicited opinions are being thrown around, I might as well offer mine."

"Shut up."

"Now, c'mon, Malcolm, we're friends and all, but when I'm in uniform you can't go telling me to shut up."

"We're veering off the subject," I said.

"Listen, Jason, I appreciate your concern for my daughter," said Malcolm. "I really do. But it's easy for you to tell me how and how not to protect her, because you don't have to deal with any of the fallout. You're just here on vacation. Any day now you'll be heading back home to work on the funny pages and whatever happens to Rachel won't be any of your concern."

"That's not true."

"Are you moving here?"

"No," I admitted.

"Are you taking her back with you?"

"No."

"So you see my point."

"Yes. I mean, no. I see your point but I don't agree with it." I needed a better angle for my argument. "There's this thing the Amish do. I don't remember what it's called; it's some sort of Amish name. But basically, when the kids reach a certain age, they go off into the world for a while and experience life outside of their own society so they can decide for themselves if they want to come back and be Amish forever. And don't quote me on this, but I think most of them decide, yeah, sin is overrated, it's the Amish life for me."

"You want Rachel to become Amish?" asked Malcolm.

"No. Not my point at all. What I'm saying is, let her go out and get a burger at a restaurant. Yeah, people will stare. Maybe they'll say some shit. So what? If Rachel decides that being locked in a shed is the way to go, fine, but it should be her decision, not yours. Don't be ruled by fear. Somebody who bashes a teenaged psychopath to death with a shovel should not be ruled by fear."

Malcolm just sat there for a while, staring at me. It was unclear from his expression if he was considering the wisdom of my idea, or if he was trying to remember where he'd left his shovel.

"I agree with him," said Sheriff Baker.

Malcolm glared at him. "Did I ask you?"

"Seriously, Malcolm, you can't keep lipping off to me like that, not while I'm on duty. It's disrespectful."

Malcolm ignored him and looked at me. "I like you, Jason. Even though you don't have a real job, I think you're all right. So I'm going to take your advice. And if my daughter gets hurt..." He trailed off, leaving me to decide for myself what might occur if his daughter were to get hurt. I could think of one pretty obvious possibility right away, and several more occurred to me quickly after that, none of which involved me remaining in a state of good health.

"She won't," I promised.

Malcolm reached into his pocket, took out a key, and tossed it to me. I caught it, which was good because it would've ended this whole conversation on a really lame note to have the key clatter to the floor.

I thanked him and walked out of the house.

Why the hell had I promised him that Rachel wouldn't get

hurt? This whole thing had started because a couple of drunken hooligans had taken me out to peep at the town legend, so of course she'd take some crap if she tried to just wander around town as if there was nothing unusual about her.

That was no reason for her not to *try* to have a normal life, though. She was a charming, witty person. Once people got to know her, they'd say, "*Wow, we should've started hanging out with Rachel Kramer long ago.*"

What about her old friends? Surely they hadn't all purposely abandoned her. Malcolm had probably just scared them off. Or they moved away from home, which I suppose is what kids tended to do after high school, especially if they lived in a small town like this. If Rachel gave me some names, I'd try to track them down.

Sure, it probably wasn't my place to barge into town and tell Malcolm and Rachel how to live their lives, but I didn't care. If Rachel truly wanted to stay hidden away from the rest of the world, fine. I couldn't grab her by the leg and drag her kicking and screaming into society. (Mostly because she'd break free and then kick my ass.) But talking to Malcolm had set the foundation for fixing a really screwed up situation, and maybe they'd just needed an outsider's perspective.

I walked over to the shed and knocked on the door.

"Dad?" asked Rachel.

"Nope. It's me."

"I'm glad he didn't shoot you."

"Me too."

"Did you come back to say goodbye?"

"Nope." I reached out and rattled the padlock with my index finger. "I've got the key."

"You stole it?"

"No. He gave it to me willingly."

"Are you serious?"

"Yes indeed."

"Are you a Jedi?"

"I'm just persuasive. Is it okay if I unlock it?"

"Yes, of course."

I unlocked the padlock and removed it. I wanted to fling it into the woods, but decided that was a little too extreme. Rachel opened the door, not wearing her mask. "Are you sure you haven't come to burn my place down?"

"Nope. Got that out of my system."

"Then, please, come in."

I followed her inside, and we both sat down at her table.

"I'm sorry about all of this," said Rachel. "I know it's weird. I hope you don't think less of my dad for locking me in here. He's just trying to keep me safe."

"In the spirit of true honesty, yeah, I do kind of think less of him. Locking you in here is a dick move."

"He knows that if I really wanted to, I could bash the door down. It's not a high-tech security system."

I set the padlock on the table. "You should throw this away. Just fling it as far as you can."

"He could buy another one pretty easily. Lots of places sell padlocks. They're not an obscure item."

"I know, but it's symbolic."

"Jason, though you're being very sweet, I think you're making this into a bigger deal than it is."

I shrugged. "Maybe I am. Let's both make this into a bigger deal than it is. Just go on outside and hurl that thing like it was an Olympic event. Not through your dad's window or anything, but as far as you can in the other direction."

Rachel smiled. "I'll think about it."

"Would you like to get lunch?" I asked.

"Peanut butter sandwiches?"

"No, I mean go out for lunch. Can I take you out to lunch?"

Rachel's smile disappeared. "No, you may not."

"Why not?"

"Don't be naïve."

"I'm not worried if you're not."

"Oh, well, I'm so relieved to hear that you're not worried. Because this will be so much more difficult for *you*."

"That's not what I meant. I just think we should go out for a burger."

"I don't like to go out."

"You don't like to go out, or your father doesn't like you to go out?"

"I don't like to have people gape at me."

"What if I wear a really, really stupid hat? Everybody will be saying 'Who's that dipshit with the hat?' Nobody will be looking at you."

"Do you really think the solution to my self-esteem issues is to be seen with an older man in a dumb hat?"

"C'mon. A delicious burger. If you're not enjoying yourself, we'll leave, I promise."

"I don't know."

"Do it for me. My agent has probably put a hit out on me, so this may be my last meal. Won't you grant a poor cartoonist the favor of bringing some joy to the final burger he'll ever eat? You don't want me to die alone, do you? Nobody should have to die alone."

"You won't be alone," said Rachel. "The assassin will be there with you."

"Fair enough. But what if it's a distance kill?"

"If it's a distance kill, then you're recklessly endangering my life by asking me to go out with you, and you deserve to die alone."

"That's sound logic. What if there was no hit man, and I'd just made it up because I was trying to be cute? Let's pretend that you weren't responding to my sincere tone, so I'd switched gears and gone for silliness. If I switched back to sincerity, would you go get a burger with me?"

"Probably not."

"I'd really like you to let me take you out to lunch."

Rachel shook her head.

"I'd really, really like you to let me take you out to lunch."

"Why don't you go get the burgers, and we'll eat them here?"

"I'd really, really, really like you to let me take you out to lunch."

"Are you just going to keep adding 'reallys' until I cave?"

"Possibly."

"What peer pressure is next? Drugs?"

"No."

"Sex?"

"I'm just trying to buy you a hamburger and fries."

"Do you promise we can leave whenever I want?"

"Absolutely."

"Even if we haven't gotten our burgers yet?"

"Yes."

I felt bad for being so damned pushy, but this was important, right? Friends make friends do things they don't want to do if it's in their best interest. When I was in college, my roommate didn't want to call this girl he'd met at a party, and I put the phone in his hand and dialed for him. That night, I had to listen while they had clumsy, unsatisfying sex, but it was still sex, and my roommate thanked me in the morning. Sometimes we just need a little push.

"Okay," said Rachel.

CHAPTER ELEVEN

Rachel and I sat in a booth in the same restaurant where Chuck had stated his disapproval of my recent behavior. There weren't many dining choices in Lake Gladys. A few other people were in the restaurant, including a couple of teenagers, but it still felt like we had a decent amount of privacy. Rachel wasn't wearing a mask.

"See?" I said. "This isn't so bad."

"Every single person in this restaurant is avoiding looking at me."

"So what if they are?"

"I'm making people want to puke."

"No, you're not."

"I'm not enjoying myself. You said we could go."

"You don't want to at least try the burger?"

"I've had their burgers many times," said Rachel. "In the comfort of my own home."

"All right, let's get out of here."

Rachel glanced around the restaurant, then sighed. "Hot fries would be nice."

The server, a blonde woman in her thirties with gratuity-enhancing cleavage, walked over to our booth. I was prepared to give her crap if she stared at Rachel ("*Why don't you take a picture? It'll last longer*," but wittier) but instead she smiled at both of us, took our orders, and said she'd be right back with our drinks.

"I freaked her out," said Rachel.

"No, you didn't."

"Did you see her face?"

"You ordered the Double Belly Burster Bacon Cheeseburger. She was reacting to that."

"If I'm going to be this uncomfortable, I'm going to have the biggest burger on the menu."

"I'm all for it, but you have to understand how ordering a cheeseburger of that size is going to affect some people."

"Maybe if I increase my ass size enough, nobody will look at my face."

"It's possible."

"I wish I'd brought my mask."

"No, you don't."

"Yes, I do."

"The mask is creepy."

"But it doesn't mess with people's appetite."

"You're not messing with anybody's appetite."

"I'm going out to the car to get my mask."

"I'll get it for you," I offered.

The server set down our drinks, smiled, and left.

"You're lucky I'm distracted," said Rachel, before taking a sip of her chocolate milkshake. "Oh, yeah, this is good stuff. I forgot what they're like when they're not melted."

"See, you could have one of these every day," I said. "And it would help with your ass-expansion strategy."

"Did you just think of that?"

"No, I've been waiting for years to use my 'ass-expansion strategy' line. Every time I start a conversation I think, *this could be the one*, but it's never worked out for me. You can imagine my frustration."

"You poor thing." Rachel took another long sip of her shake. She was downing that thing at an alarming rate, but I didn't say anything, because despite the light teasing, I knew there was an invisible line that should not be crossed in reference to the quantity of calories consumed by a woman during a particular meal.

"I made it up on the spot," I told her. "I'm very clever."

"You should put it in a strip."

"I really should. I haven't had a good controversy since I broke that kid's arm earlier this month."

We chatted for a while longer, and Rachel didn't talk about her mask anymore. Her eyes lit up as the server brought out her burger, which didn't look like it could be eaten without the restaurant patron unhinging their jaw. We told the server that no, we didn't need anything else, everything looked wonderful, and then we took our first bites, chewing silently in bliss.

I finally spoke. "Good stuff, huh?"

"Best burger I've had in five years."

"I agree."

"So why do you like me?"

"Because you're cool."

"Okay, that's really, really lame. I'm serious. I don't feel like this is just a pity party."

"It's not."

"Then what is it?"

"Friends going out for a burger. That's what friends do."

"Let's say we were in your hometown, where everybody knows you. Would you still go out for a burger with me?"

I didn't even have to think about it. "Yes."

"What if *Entertainment Tonight* came to your house to do a feature on you? Would you let them interview me as one of your friends?"

"Sure. And it could happen, because *Entertainment Tonight* does sooooo very many cartoonist spotlights."

"I'm sorry. I guess you're not the only one who can be needy."

One of the teenagers, looking at us, whispered something to his friend, who snickered. I tried to ignore it and returned my attention to Rachel.

"I've dated far needier women."

"Are we dating now?" She popped a french fry into her mouth, then smiled at my startled expression. "I was kidding."

"I know."

"You looked terrified."

"I didn't look terrified."

"You were stricken with horror, as if Satan himself had said '*Be my eternal bitch.*'"

"You're right. I'm a commitment-phobe. My last twelve relationships ended with me jumping out of third-story windows to escape."

"Does it spook you out when I joke about us having a relationship? I'll stop doing it if it does."

"Nope. Doesn't spook me out."

"Liar."

"I'm serious!"

"It's not some kind of...I don't know, burn victim fetish or anything, is it?"

"Does that fetish even exist?"

"If it does, you can send them my way."

"You are a weird, weird person," I informed her.

"I've developed a lot of defense mechanisms."

"Well, all I have to say is: stop questioning my motives, or you're paying for your own burger."

Rachel smiled. "Okay, I'll stop. I don't know how to behave anymore. My conversations these days are either with my dad or my owls, and they both suck at talking."

The teenagers walked toward our booth on their way out of the restaurant. As they passed, one of them muttered something that I'm pretty sure was "*No wonder they keep her locked up.*"

"Hey!" I said.

The teenager stopped.

"Apologize for that."

"It's okay," Rachel assured me.

"No, it's not." I looked the teenager in the eye to make sure he knew I was serious. "Tell my friend you're sorry."

"Hey, I paid for my lunch, too. I shouldn't have to look at that while I'm eating."

"I'm only going to—"

"No, Jason, it's okay," said Rachel. "I understand. I know how difficult it is to eat when you're watching—" She contorted her face and spoke in a mock-demonic voice. "*—a horrible deformed creature, who lurks under your bed at night and wants to devour your flesh and suck out your eyebaaaaaaalllllls!*"

She roared like a hideous monster.

The teenagers ran for the exit as fast as they could. It was a wonderful, glorious thing to witness. I hoped that neither of them would trip and break an arm. (Although I'll admit that this was not a passionate hope.) The one who got to the door first pulled it open and accidentally smacked his friend with it, adding to my delight.

I was laughing so hard that I suddenly had a very real concern that I was going to choke on my bite of hamburger. I began to cough yet couldn't stop laughing. The sight of those creeps running away would almost be worth having my windpipe explode through my throat, but I hoped to stave off death this afternoon.

I took a drink of water, coughed a few more times, and decided that I was not going to choke to death. I wiped my eyes. "That was brilliant. You're a mad genius. I can't believe you didn't want to go out today!"

Then I noticed that Rachel was crying.

"Aw, shit, I'm sorry," I told her. I pulled a napkin from the dispenser and handed it to her. She sniffled and dabbed at her eyes. "Do you want to leave?"

"Yes."

The server walked over to our table. "Hey, I apologize for that. They aren't bad kids; just a little obnoxious sometimes. Can I get you anything?"

"Nah, just the check," I said.

"Do you want to-go containers?"

I looked over at Rachel. She shook her head.

"No, thank you," I said.

The server left. Every time kids ran screaming in terror, it worked out badly for me. I was sure that Rachel would find this hilarious in retrospect, but I hoped that "retrospect" wasn't a ninety-year-old Rachel cackling over the memory in her nursing home.

Rachel blew her nose into the napkin. "I ruined lunch," she said.

"No, you didn't."

"I'm sitting here crying. I think lunch is ruined."

"It's not. Not for me, anyway."

Rachel pulled several more napkins out of the dispenser. "This is why I don't go anywhere."

"Do you cry when you're sitting all alone?"

"Sometimes."

"So, you might as well be enjoying an un-melted milkshake while you're doing it."

"Everybody's staring at us."

"Yeah, because they're amused by your zombie impression. They're all on your side."

"Including the person who burned down your cabin?"

"That was probably rats chewing through the wiring."

"Do you really believe that?"

"I think it's irrelevant to what's happening here. Look, we were having a perfectly fine lunch, and some kids made a rotten comment, and you wreaked vengeance upon them. I enjoyed the hell out of it. Sure, I'll reluctantly agree that in the future, your reaction should be more subdued, but you didn't ruin anything. You made it better."

Rachel blew her nose again. "I'm completely humiliated."

"You shouldn't be."

The server returned with the check and a couple of chocolate chip cookies on a plate. "On the house," she said, giving Rachel a sympathetic smile.

"See?" I asked Rachel. "Nobody ever gives *me* free cookies."

Actually, that wasn't true. I'd done various interviews where they had refreshments available, including cookies, but nobody in a restaurant had ever given me free chocolate chip cookies, so I think the point was still valid.

I left an extra large tip for the server, which I supposed could have been her motivation for the cookies, and then paid our bill at the register up front. I was grateful that Rachel didn't rush out of the restaurant, although she kept her head down, staring at the floor.

We returned to my car. She picked up her mask from the seat before getting in, then rested it on her lap as she buckled her seat belt.

Some guy was standing in the parking lot, a few cars away, not even pretending that he wasn't staring at us. He was skinny, with curly brown hair, and looked about twenty-two or twenty-three. Rachel's age.

I hoped Rachel wouldn't notice him, but she did. She quickly looked away.

"You know him?" I asked.

Rachel nodded.

"Ex-boyfriend?"

"No, no. Allen. Brandon's best friend."

"Ah." I peered at him more closely. Allen did kind of look like somebody who'd be friends with a date-raping psychopath. That was an unfair assessment of me to make, so I didn't say it out loud. "I guess he's not somebody who'd be happy to see you again."

"Nope."

If I had to make a list of arson suspects, the best friend of the guy who'd savaged Rachel's face was a reasonable candidate. Although I supposed that if I'd burned down somebody's cabin, I wouldn't be standing there staring at them in a restaurant parking lot like a creepy-ass stalker. I'd at least get a pair of binoculars and watch from a distance.

I wouldn't say anything now, but if I saw him lurking around again, I'd mention it to Sheriff Baker.

"Where do you want to go now?" I asked, as we drove away from the restaurant.

"Home."

"You sure?"

"Yes."

"All right."

I'd promised I'd take her home if she asked, so I guessed I had to stick to it. I was relieved that she didn't put the mask on, but as we drove back to her place, we didn't say much of anything.

CHAPTER TWELVE

A s I turned onto her road, Rachel said, "You know what? That was stupid of me."

"What?"

"Getting so upset. I should've ignored those idiots."

"It's no big deal."

"At the very least, I should've let the waitress give us a to-go box. You were nice and took me out to lunch, and I wasted most of that delicious burger. I'm sorry."

"Don't apologize."

"No, I'm really sorry. You were brave enough to be seen in public having lunch with Blister, and I screwed it all up. I acted like a baby."

"I swear to you, it's okay. No problem at all. I'd be self-conscious too."

Shit! Was that a horrible thing to say? Had my mouth just outpaced my brain?

Fortunately, Rachel didn't seem to notice. "Don't pull into my driveway just yet," she said.

"Okay." I stopped the car.

"I know I'm unpleasant to look at."

"You're not—"

"*Please* don't deny that. I'm hideous. I have a lot of good qualities, but please don't make things up that you think I want to hear. What I'm saying is that I know I'm unpleasant to look at, and ever since I came home from the hospital it's been easier to hide away than deal with the staring and whispering. Yeah, my dad forbade me to go out in public, but he couldn't have stopped me if I really wanted to leave. I could have done whatever the hell I wanted, and what I wanted to do was to sit in a goddamn shed with a bunch of owl pictures."

She paused as if waiting for me to comment, but I couldn't think of anything to say except that I liked her owl pictures, which would've been a dumb thing to say, so I remained silent. Finally she turned toward me.

"I'm not going to keep apologizing for ruining our meal. I just want to say that I really, truly appreciate how nice you've been to me, and I'd very much like to have lunch with you again, this time without me threatening to eat anybody's eyeballs."

"It's a deal."

I couldn't quite interpret the look she gave me. Then I realized that she was leaning toward me, and my sudden reaction was, *oh, shit, what's she doing?*

I didn't pull away, exactly, but I think she could see in my eyes that I *really* wasn't expecting this, because she immediately sat up straight again.

"Okay," she said, "we can go into my driveway now."

"Rachel, wait—"

"The driveway is good."

"I don't think your dad is ready for this to be anything more than friends having lunch. I think his head would explode."

Rachel nodded. "I understand. He's a scary man."

"I just...I think you're great. I just think that it was difficult enough to gain his trust up to this point, and we should stick to baby steps."

"Do you need baby steps, or do you think my dad needs baby steps?"

I didn't have an immediate response.

"It's fine," she said. "I one hundred percent get it. Can we move past the awkwardness and pretend this never happened? I slipped. I tipped over a bit in my seat. Very clumsy of me."

"I just don't want to piss your dad off."

"I said, I completely understand. His opinion is what's important."

"Now, Rachel, let's be fair. One hour ago I was trying to talk your dad out of keeping a padlock on your door. I'm an adult and you're an adult, but it's not a stretch to think that he'd go absolutely batshit homicidal insane if he thought I was taking advantage of you. Right?"

"Yes. You're right. You're completely right." Rachel didn't sound like she was being sarcastic. "I don't know what I was thinking. I'm not good at picking up on social cues. I'm sorry."

"Don't apologize."

"Can we pretend this never happened?"

"We don't have to pretend it never happened," I said.

"I'd like to, though."

"It's totally fine. This changes nothing. Don't worry about it."

"You're sweating."

"So?"

"Just an observation."

Yeah, I was sweating. Because I felt like this conversation could easily veer into her asking me if I would have kissed her if her father's intense disapproval weren't an issue. Would I? Or would I have flinched?

I probably would have flinched.

Had she looked like a supermodel, I still would have avoided the kiss, because the whole Malcolm issue was a genuinely good reason to take things more slowly. I wasn't using that as an excuse. But hypothetically, in a world where Malcolm was a jovial guy who was trying to marry his daughter off in exchange for a couple of cows, what would I have done?

I'm not superficial about looks, but I'm also not blind. There's a point where you have to ask, am I cool with the idea of waking up next to that every morning? As much as I *liked* Rachel, I wasn't attracted to her.

We all have a type. Maybe disfigured girls just weren't mine.

"Look, Rachel, you're—"

"If you say, 'Rachel, you're a very nice girl,' I'll rip your dick off."

"That's not what I was going to say."

"If you say a variation on it, I'll rip your dick off."

"Please don't."

"Then don't say it. Don't say anything patronizing."

"There's a difference between patronizing and reassuring."

"You lose a dick either way."

"Okay, well, I don't want that to happen. But it would be easier to move past this if we talk about it."

"I understand that. I'm not feeling very rational right now. What would help me move past this is if we pulled into my driveway."

Now it kind of sounded like she was mad at me. That was always tricky territory with women, and it was worse with Rachel because her face didn't convey the subtle expressions that would serve as a cue that I'd entered the danger zone. I decided that my best bet was to drop her off.

We pulled into her driveway. Malcolm was sitting on his porch, and I was relieved that he didn't have a shotgun in his lap. We couldn't continue our conversation with him sitting there watching us, so I supposed this was the end for now.

"I really did have a good time," I told her.

"Me too," said Rachel, unconvincingly.

"Lunch tomorrow?"

"I don't think so."

"We don't have to go anywhere. I'll bring something."

"I don't know. Probably. We'll see."

Rachel opened her door. She tried to get out, but hadn't unfastened her seatbelt.

"You need to—" I started to say.

"I know." She released the seatbelt and got out. "I'll talk to you tomorrow," she said.

"Sounds good."

I waved to Malcolm, who didn't wave back, then backed out of the driveway and drove away.

Okay, well, that sucked.

I wasn't sure what I'd been expecting. It wasn't as if Rachel was going to say, "*Goodness, the world is a magical place, full of smiling faces and whimsy! Thank you for unlocking its potential!*" I just didn't think it would be a complete disaster.

I felt bad for leading Rachel on. Usually it was the guys who were surprised to just be friends. I'd probably been a little flirty and that was wrong. She'd been trapped in a frickin' shed for five years; it wasn't okay to mess with her emotions like that.

Yep, the handsome cartoonist should've made it easier for the young woman to resist his charms. How irresponsible of me.

Being attracted to her would be insane. I was open-minded, but there were limits. Friends, yes. Lovers, nope. Some things are too weird.

Which did not explain why, in the absence of a cabin on the lake, I was still here. Why was I staying here instead of just going home? My Chuck-imposed exile had been lifted. There was no reason for me to still be hanging out at Lake Gladys except for Rachel.

I couldn't name any other friends where I'd be willing to stay in a cheap motel just so I could meet them for burgers. With anybody else, it would've been, "*Sorry, arsonist took out the cabin, gotta cancel our lunch plans.*"

Sure, there was the whole element of swooping in there like some big hero who rescued the damsel from her overprotective father, but I was thirty-eight years old and had not thus far been predisposed toward putting my personal safety at risk for people I'd just met.

Why was I still here?

Pity?

Moral outrage?

Deep, depressing loneliness?

I was usually pretty good about getting into my own head. I'd married Vivian because she was smart and pretty and was nice to me back when I was an inept bumbling doofus who dreamed of drawing comics for a living. I'd dated Melissa because I was angry and bitter after my divorce and she was angry and bitter after her divorce and somehow our anger and bitterness seemed compatible. I'd dated Jennifer because she had a spectacular ass, and by that point I'd reached a level of success where I could attract women with spectacular asses. Pretty much every relationship after that was based on the level of hotness, which probably explained why they were all short-lived.

I'd never sat around and wondered why I was behaving in such a way. My motives were always pretty transparent. It made absolutely no sense that I didn't just get in the car and drive back home. There was no reason for me to stay in this bizarre situation. Why didn't I return to my normal life?

I should. I really should. This was ridiculous. The vacation was over as soon as the cabin went inferno.

I went back to the motel and packed my suitcase. I checked out at the front desk, put Ignatz into the car, and drove away.

Wait, was I really going to drive away without saying goodbye to Rachel? That was some romantic comedy bullshit. I'd at least have to explain to her that my vacation was over.

Of course, if I went back there so soon, it would look like I was fleeing. I should wait until this evening before I sped out of Lake Gladys, just so I didn't hurt her feelings.

So, what, I was going to hang out here for a few more hours to make it seem like our disappointing lunch and my departure weren't related? Who did that sort of thing? What was the matter with me?

I should just go. I could look up Malcolm's number tomorrow and call to let Rachel know there'd been a cartooning emergency and I had to leave. She'd understand.

That sounded kind of cowardly.

But somehow less mean than driving over there and saying, "Seeya!"

This was a weirdly difficult decision.

The most appealing option was to just return to the motel, stay another night, and have lunch with Rachel tomorrow, as planned. But that was also the deranged option. "*Sorry, Rach, I'm totally not into you, but I'm still here! No, no, it's not creepy at all.*"

What to do...what to do...what to do...

Okay, I definitely was not going to head back to her place and say goodbye, because it would make her feel terrible, like she'd driven me away.

I also definitely was not going to bide my time in Lake Gladys all afternoon, just to spare her feelings, because that was lame.

Which meant that the only option was to leave.

No, that was a terrible option.

This was making me nuts. What I needed was a legitimate reason to stay in Lake Gladys for another night. Something that actually made sense. Like, perhaps, a restaurant that served fantastic steaks, the kind that people travelled long distances to enjoy. "What did you do on your vacation, Jason?" "Oh, man, I had this amazing steak dinner!" "Wow, sounds like a great vacation! Wish I'd been there!"

Yes, somehow I'd reached the point of mental instability where I was making up excuses to justify my actions to *my own brain.*

Lake Gladys was not good for me.

I was leaving.

I drove for about an hour, feeling at peace with my decision.

Then I turned around and drove back.

CHAPTER THIRTEEN

T hough the cabin was history, the lake itself had not been consumed in an inferno, so I decided to go out on the paddleboat for a while. When I parked in front of the rubble, Sheriff Baker and a man in a white dress shirt and tie were there. I rolled the windows down so Ignatz could have fresh air, then got out of the car.

Sheriff Baker smiled and waved at me. "How's it going?"

"Not bad," I said. "Figured I'd enjoy the lake while I'm still in town."

"Oh, sure, sure. This gentleman is just checking things out for the insurance company. You know, making sure nobody burned down the place to collect some cash."

The man nodded politely at me.

"Does it look like arson?" I asked.

Sheriff Baker shrugged. "It would've been nice if they left a can of gasoline around or something. There are ways to tell, burn patterns and so on, but that's really more of a big-city thing."

"We can tell," said the man. He didn't seem like somebody

you'd want to invite to a party unless you'd already given up on it.

"Well, I'll leave you to it," I said. "Let me know if you need anything."

I went out to the dock, got in the paddleboat, and paddled out to the center of the lake. Then I just floated for a while, enjoying the sunshine and the silence. After about fifteen minutes, Sheriff Baker and the insurance guy got in their separate cars and drove away.

Ah, it was so nice out here. So peaceful.

This is why I was still here. The lake. Nothing else.

I closed my eyes.

I nodded off.

I opened my eyes again when a family in a motorboat sped past me. I wasn't sure how long I'd been asleep, but my arms had acquired a delightfully attractive sunburn. You'd think that with Rachel's burnt face and the fate of the cabin, I'd be more aware of the need for sunscreen, but, nope, my bright red skin was proof that I was a moron. Oh well.

Somebody was standing on Chuck's dock.

I was too far away to say for certain, but I was pretty sure that it was the guy who'd been watching us in the parking lot. Brandon's buddy. Adam? No, Allen.

He was using the same *modus operandi* of just standing there staring like a creepy bastard. Didn't he realize that being all spooky could make him an arson suspect?

As I paddled back in, he stayed where he was. Even as I paddled right up to the dock, he didn't move. He just kept watching me.

"Hi there," I said.

"Hello."

I paddled until the boat scraped against the bottom of the lake, then got out and dragged it onto the shore. "Can I help you with something?"

Allen shrugged.

"Just figured you'd stand there and gaze upon my beauty?" I asked.

"Something like that."

I stepped out onto the dock. "I saw you before. Whatever you're doing isn't as endearing as you think it is."

"Why are you here?" he asked.

"I'm on vacation."

"But why here?"

"Because this is where my agent sent me for some down time after I acted out. You have a fine little town here. Interesting people. Clear water. So now let's circle this conversation back to my original question: can I help you with something?"

"People are tired of you being here."

"Are they?"

"Yeah."

"Well, if you talk to people, tell them I said hi."

Allen narrowed his eyes. "Are you making fun of me?"

"No. I'm a professional humorist. When I make fun of you, you'll know it. I'd do it now but I don't work for free."

Allen's eyes narrowed even further, as if he still wasn't sure if he was being made fun of or not. "We're ready for you to leave," he said.

"Let's put everything out in the open," I said. "You're mad because I'm spending time with Rachel Kramer, right?"

"That's right."

"Well, it's none of your business, so if you want to fuck off, that'd be appreciated. Go on, just fuck right off back to wherever you came from." I used my index and middle fingers to mimic a pair of legs walking away.

"I'm not going anywhere."

"You're trespassing. This is my agent's property."

"Are you going to call the sheriff?"

"If you make me."

Allen didn't move. "She's disgusting."

"Why? Because her face got burnt up? She doesn't have an infectious disease. If somebody did that to you, would you want people to call you disgusting?"

"How can you even look at her?"

"I can look at her fine. When I look at you, not gonna lie, I get a little queasy. My stomach is churning just a bit. I'm not sure how to explain it. Maybe I have an aversion to looking at assholes." I took a step toward him. "Oh, by the way, now I'm making fun of you."

Allen looked down at his feet and muttered something.

"What was that?" I asked.

"I said, you need to leave."

"It's not going to happen."

"You'll be sorry."

"Actually, my vacation was over. I was all packed up and ready to leave. But because you're being so whiny, I may just buy some property around here, build a lakeside amusement park."

I was probably taking this too far. I was certain I could kick this guy's ass if he actually tried to make this physical, but my hands were crucial to my livelihood, and the last thing I needed was to be unable to draw new strips while my fingers healed from breaking against his jaw.

"I'm not trying to be antagonistic," I said. "I understand that bad things happened and you lost your best friend. But you're mad at the wrong person. Be mad at Brandon, wherever he is."

"I am."

"Good."

"I've got plenty of anger to go around."

"Well, it's misplaced. You should get to know Rachel. You'd like her."

"I already knew her."

"Right. You would have. Best friend's girlfriend. Sorry. All I'm saying is that none of this is her fault."

Allen chuckled. "None of it, huh?"

"That's right."

"Whatever."

"Are you saying that she slashed up her own face?"

"I'm saying that maybe she deserved it."

"Okay, well, thank you for this insight into your moral compass. My invitation to fuck right off still stands."

Allen stepped toward me. I wasn't sure if it was a threatening step in my direction, or if he was simply ready to leave the dock and I was in his way. I moved aside, hoping it was the latter.

He walked past me.

He stepped off the dock, then turned back to face me. "You're not leaving, huh?"

"Not presently."

"Okay."

"Did you burn down the cabin?" I asked.

"Maybe."

"Maybe? What the hell does that mean?"

"You don't know the definition of the word 'maybe'?" Allen grinned. "Now I'm making fun of you."

"Are you seriously going to make me call the sheriff on you?"

"I'm not making you do anything. Apparently you live in a world where anybody can do whatever they want." And with that, the little shit walked away.

I wanted to rush after him and punch him in the face, but again, my hands were the instruments of my trade. I found it hard to believe that somebody would burn down Chuck's cabin and then "maybe" admit to it, but I was going to call Sheriff Baker anyway.

I drove to Rachel's place. I was so angry that I was muttering to myself, which wasn't something I did very often, and I was clutching the steering wheel so tightly that my fingers ached. I wished I'd picked up a canoe paddle and knocked that creep into the lake. Who did he think he was? What was wrong with this town? I probably *should* bring Rachel with me, so she could live someplace where everybody wasn't a complete freaking nutcase.

Goddamn, I was mad.

I think even Ignatz could sense it. He sat on the passenger seat, head hung.

I pulled into the driveway and got out of my car. I decided to visit Malcolm first, because I wasn't sure if Rachel had a phone.

When he answered the door, Malcolm didn't look angry or annoyed. Instead, he seemed resigned to my continued presence in his life, like taxes.

"Do you know a kid named Allen?" I asked. "Brandon's best friend."

Malcolm nodded. "Not well, but yeah, I've been around him a few times. Any friend of Brandon's is an enemy of mine, so I can't say that I've gone out of my way to be nice to him."

"He doesn't seem to like your daughter very much."

"I wouldn't expect him to, but what makes you say that?"

"He was watching us at the restaurant, and then he showed up at the cabin."

"I thought it burned down?"

"It did. I was just using the lake. He basically told me that Rachel was disgusting and that I needed to leave. I asked him if he torched the cabin and he said maybe. I don't think he did, but I definitely want to let Sheriff Baker know to keep an eye on this guy."

"Phone's in the kitchen. If Allen shows up here, he'd better *pray* that somebody from law enforcement is also here."

I went into the kitchen and made the call. Sheriff Baker assured me that he'd be headed right out to ask Allen some questions and make sure he didn't bother Rachel or me again.

"Can we get a restraining order?" I asked.

"Did he specifically threaten you?"

"No, he didn't specifically threaten me with physical violence, but it was definitely a 'get out of town or something bad will happen' visit."

"I'll put a scare into him," Sheriff Baker assured me. "He's not a bad guy. People around here just aren't used to things getting shaken up. If you see him watching you again, even if he doesn't say anything to you, let me know and we'll get a judge to slap a restraining order on him."

"Thanks."

I didn't feel that much better after I hung up. Obviously, they couldn't just throw Allen in jail, and even I didn't believe that he was legitimately dangerous. But it truly pissed me off that he thought he could wander onto Chuck's dock and tell me to get out of town.

It was nobody's business what I did with Rachel.

I wanted to kick something. Desperately. Unfortunately, I didn't think Malcolm would be okay with me kicking his wall or his possessions, so I just stood there, clenching and unclenching my hands into fists.

"You look perturbed," said Malcolm.

"Very perturbed."

"Got some aggression you need to vent?"

"Yeah. Big-time."

Malcolm smiled. "Want to chop up some firewood for me?"

"Actually, yes. That would be lovely."

I stood outside with an axe, hoping that Malcolm wasn't watching just how much I sucked at chopping wood. It wasn't that my arms were too puny; apparently there was some kind of art to it, because though I felt like I was slamming into the wood with the force of a mighty lumberjack, the wood was not splitting apart as if a mighty lumberjack had struck it.

Also, I completely missed a couple of times, which was embarrassing.

"Dad has you doing chores?" asked Rachel, startling me so badly that I almost dropped the axe.

I turned around. She was wearing the light blue mask.

"Nah," I said. "Blowing off some steam."

"Have you read *The Wonderful Wizard of Oz*?" she asked.

"No, I've only seen the movie."

"In the book, the Tin Man's origin story is that he keeps chopping off his own limbs while he swings his axe, and replacing them with metal ones, until he's completely dismembered and made of tin."

"Are you saying that my axe-swinging skills are going to take me in that direction?"

"Just an observation."

I swung the axe again, hoping for an impressive hit that would split a log completely in half. The blade made it about a quarter of the way through, but at least I didn't miss. I lifted the axe, taking the log with it, and slammed it against the tree stump again. Three more hits later, and the log was halved.

Rachel applauded.

"Thank you," I said.

"Seriously, why are you chopping firewood?"

"Because I can either slam this axe into a log and be productive, or I can slam it into Allen's skull, which would be even more productive but also illegal."

"What happened?"

"He tried to be all menacing. I'm over it now, though." I set down the axe.

"You don't look over it."

"Do you have any crayons? Maybe if I drew a picture of his face on the log it would do the trick."

"I do, actually."

"No, I'm just kidding. But I'll take a Cherry Coke if you still have them."

"Of course."

She walked back to the shed. I decided to follow her.

My hands were tingling. I should've been wearing gloves.

I couldn't get over that piece of crap telling me what to do. Malcolm? Fine, okay. Rachel was his daughter. He was trying to protect her. It was severely misguided but you could understand his rationale. But Allen? Friend of the monster who ruined her life in the first place? He should've been *thrilled* that somebody was being nice to Rachel. He should've been ecstatic that in some tiny way, the damage done by the psychopath he'd befriended was being undone.

I agreed with Malcolm. If Allen showed up here, he'd better hope that Sheriff Baker was also here to keep things from getting bloody.

"You okay?" Rachel asked me, as she opened her door.

"Yes."

"You sure?"

"Who the hell does he think he is?"

"I'm getting the impression that you don't like people telling you what to do."

"You are absolutely right."

After we walked inside, I pulled Rachel into my arms, took off her mask, and kissed her.

CHAPTER FOURTEEN

Rachel put her arms around me and returned the kiss, but it wasn't with quite the same level of passion so I adjusted accordingly. Her lips were hard and rough but the sensation was not remotely unpleasant. It felt like exactly the right thing to be doing.

She pulled away. Had I just made a gigantic blunder?

Then she glanced at the door. Oh. Right. The door was still open. If Malcolm was watching through the window, he could see right in.

Rachel pushed the door closed.

She smiled. "Why did you do that?"

"I wanted to."

"That's a perfectly good reason." She gave me a gentle kiss.

"Why did you try to kiss me in the car?" I asked.

"I was trying to take advantage of you."

"Good reason." We kissed again. I felt way less angry now.

I wasn't sure where I should be trying to steer this. I kind of wanted to scoop her up in my arms and walk her over to the bed (which was not far to walk, so my back would be fine), but I wasn't getting a *"take me now, you stud"* vibe. We had salvaged the previous awkwardness and I didn't want to mess things up again.

So we just kissed some more. Gently. Tenderly. No tongue.

I wasn't checking my watch, but after a while I realized that if Malcolm was going to pound down the door, he would have done it by now. He either hadn't seen us or he wasn't going to intervene.

A flick of tongue from Rachel. Then she pulled away and started giggling.

"What?"

"This is just so ridiculous."

"Why?"

"Because you're old and I'm hideous." She put a hand over her mouth to stifle the giggles, but couldn't keep them contained.

"I'm not ninety! Thirty-eight is a perfectly respectable age to be dating a twenty-three year-old. When I'm fifty-eight, you'll be forty-three."

"And?"

"Fifty-eight year-olds date forty-three year-olds all the time. It's as socially acceptable as you can get."

Rachel took her hand away from her mouth. She was smiling but not giggling. "Are we dating now?"

"I don't know," I said. "Maybe we're just making out. I'm cool with it either way."

"What would your friends think if they saw you now?"

"'*Woooo! Go for it, Jason!*'"

"You lie."

"I lie not."

"They would be gaping at you in horror."

"No, they wouldn't, and if they did, I'd kick their asses, no matter how long we'd been friends. If we're going to date, we have to work on some of your self-esteem issues."

"Will you take me to a fancy restaurant?"

"Yes."

"Will you take me to meet your parents?"

"No, but only because they're dead. If they were alive, yes."

She kissed me. "Thank you for pretending."

"I'm not pretending."

"Thank you anyway." She pulled away and walked over to the portable refrigerator. She took out two Cherry Cokes and handed one to me.

I opened the can and took a long drink. The wood chopping and rage had made me thirsty. She sat down at the table, so I did the same.

"Thanks for being my friend," she said.

"Anytime."

"When are you going back home?"

"I don't know. Not this afternoon, I can promise you that."

"But you can't stay here forever."

"No, I can't. But I'm not that far. Three and a half hours. And it doesn't matter where I draw as long as I meet my deadlines, so there's no reason I can't come back and visit all the time. We can make this work."

Rachel popped open her own can of soda. She took a sip, set down the can, picked it up again, took another sip, then set it down again. "I guess I just don't understand why you're doing this."

"I like you. I liked you from the moment you said it was hilarious that I broke that kid's arm."

"I like you, too."

"Do you want me to be superficial? I can do that. You have a fantastic body. You have an amazing, tight, scorching-hot body."

"I do keep in shape."

"Do you want the full truth?"

"Yes."

"When I saw your face in the window that first night, it scared the shit out of me. I thought I was watching a real live horror movie. And when I came over to apologize and you took off your mask, I understood why you wore it."

Rachel's eyes glistened with tears.

"Don't cry," I said. "That's the bad stuff that leads to the good stuff."

"Okay."

"So, to recap, yes, when I see a girl whose face has been slashed up with a straight razor and burnt with a blowtorch, my initial reaction is shock and unease. That's just the way it works. Then I got to know you, and you're incredible, and your appearance doesn't matter anymore."

Since I did not expect to get laid this afternoon, I realized (but did not share with Rachel) that I wasn't saying this to get laid. I truly believed it. Her looks *didn't* matter anymore.

Was there also an element of "*Screw you, world, and especially you, Allen—I'll do what I want!*" involved? Probably. So what?

Rachel didn't say anything, so I forged onward. "If you were a filthy dirty pig, I might not be able to get past that. But I'd be an awful person if I couldn't look past what happened to you. What if we'd been together, and *then* you were attacked? Would I have abandoned you? Not a chance in hell. I'd be proud to call you my girlfriend."

It was hard to tell, but Rachel seemed to be practically beaming.

"Okay," she said. "You can call me that, then."

We leaned across the table and kissed. That works better in the movies.

"My dad may or may not be all right with this," said Rachel. "By being my boyfriend, you're accepting the risk."

"Write up the waiver and I'll sign it."

"And we have to take things slow. Slower than you're probably used to."

"I'm fine with that."

"I'm..." Rachel took another drink to gather her courage. "I'm a virgin."

"I assumed that."

"Are you one, too?"

"Me? Uh..."

"I'm kidding. You told me you'd been married."

"Yes, I was. Although that particular marriage wasn't that much different from the virgin lifestyle."

"I assume you've been with a lot of women."

"I wouldn't say—"

"I don't want to know how many," Rachel said. "If you start to tell me, I'll put my hands over my ears and go *la la la la la*."

"That's reasonable."

"I mean it, never tell me. Even if I ask, I don't really want to know. But I won't ask so it doesn't matter. What I'm saying is that I'm sure you have plenty of experience, and I have zero experience, and it might be a long road for me to get to that point. I wanted to put that out there in case you're just after this hot bod."

"Noted."

"We can kiss as much as you want. You just can't touch my boobs or my butt. Well, you can touch my butt a little."

We kissed. I kept my hands to myself.

WHEN WE WERE DONE KISSING, which didn't happen soon, she walked me to the door. "If you're sure you want to do this, I'm going to tell my dad."

"Do you want me to tell him?" I asked.

Rachel shook her head. "I'll do it."

"Should we tell him together?"

"No. You should leave. I'll tell you how it went."

"Is it because you think he'll kill me?"

Rachel smiled. "He was never *really* going to kill you. If he got truly mad about this, the worst he'd do is yell at you. He'd yell and scream and the vein in his forehead would bulge out, and you'd *think* your life was in danger, but it wouldn't be. But I'm not trying to save you from getting yelled at. I just think this is something I should do by myself. He might respect it more coming from you. I don't care. It's important to me that I have this conversation on my terms, and let him know that it is one hundred percent something I want."

"Well, I can't argue with that," I said. "Are you sure I shouldn't just hang out here?"

"I'm sure. This might take a while. And if you're here, he'll want to talk to you instead. Come back in an hour. No, hour and a half."

"All right. Sounds good."

We kissed one last time, then she opened the door. I was ready for a steel-toed boot belonging to Malcolm to kick my teeth out, but I didn't even see Malcolm through his window.

"Oh, not to bring us down," I said, before stepping outside, "but please don't walk outside by yourself until the Allen situation is resolved."

"I won't."

She walked over to Malcolm's house, and I walked over to my car. I still kind of felt like I should stick around, but...no. Right now, anything I might say to Malcolm was irrelevant. I wasn't auditioning to be Rachel's guardian; I wanted to be her boyfriend. She needed to make her father understand that this was her decision, and she needed to do it alone.

In the spirit of pure honesty, I'll admit that when I heard the door close, I picked up my pace.

CHAPTER FIFTEEN

I was going to go not-so-silently crazy if I had to be alone with my thoughts right now. With Ignatz in the car I could pretend that I wasn't talking to myself, but until I knew how Rachel's talk with Malcolm went, I was going to be a mess. I needed human interaction to distract myself.

I supposed that I could call Chuck.

Nah. He was unlikely to lend a sympathetic ear.

It was Sunday afternoon. There might be somebody at Doug's Booze Wasteland, where this whole adventure started. A game of billiards would relax me.

"What do you think, Ignatz?" I asked. "Am I crazy?"

Ignatz offered no opinion on the matter.

I decided not to talk out loud to my dog. But was I crazy? It wasn't as if I was withering away from loneliness. My lack of a romantic partner really was just because I didn't bother to get out there and meet anybody. Even if you disregarded every other bizarre element, this was a long-distance relationship, and those rarely worked out.

I was going to start dating a twenty-three year-old disfigured virgin. Wow.

Had I really gotten over her appearance so quickly? I honestly believed that I had. I just flat-out *liked* her. I liked spending time with her. I liked talking to her. If it weren't for her face, I'd be leaping at the chance to be with her, so if I was supposedly above the concept of judging somebody based on their looks, what was stopping me?

Not a damn thing.

Well, okay, there were plenty of damn things. She was not exactly free of emotional baggage. She was fun and funny, but there had to be a lot of waking up screaming happening in that shed.

I could handle her baggage. I'd dated a woman with a moody pre-teen. This was trading up.

Was I cool with the idea that everywhere we went, people would stare at us?

I liked to think so.

And I didn't go out that much anyway. We could stay home and watch movies.

Anyway, she wanted to take it really slow. It wasn't as if she'd be moving in with me. I'd visit her here in Lake Gladys on a regular basis. See how things worked out. Keep it casual. We weren't making any lifelong commitments. If it felt weird and either of us wanted to bail, no problem. I wasn't promising her the moon.

Hell, once she got used to being out in public again, she'd probably trade me in for a younger model.

I parked in front of Doug's Booze Wasteland and went inside. The place was mostly empty, but there at the pool table was my good buddy Louie. Though Erik was nowhere to be seen, Louie had his arm around a pretty girl. I hoped it was his fiancé.

"Hi," I said, walking over and shaking his hand. "I'm Jason. We hung out a few days ago." I felt the need to remind him of this, since he'd been quite drunk.

"Yeah, yeah, I remember. This is my fiancé Holly."

"Hi, Holly."

"Hi," she said with a smirk. The smirk put a crease in the extremely generous amount of makeup that she wore.

"Can I play the winner?"

"Oh, this game's already over," said Holly. "He knocked in the eight-ball on his second turn. We're just messing around. You can play me."

I put two quarters into the slots and we started a new game. "I hear your life has been interesting since we last spoke," said Louie, as Holly racked the balls.

"What do you mean?" I asked, even though I'm not a fan of playing dumb.

"You've been hanging out with Blister, right?"

"Rachel, yeah."

Louie let out a really annoying cackle. "I can't believe you admitted it! You mean it's true?"

"Yeah, it's true," I said, suddenly not wanting to play pool anymore. "She's great. You'd like her."

"Aw, man, that's too much. Does she drool?"

"No."

"How does she even talk? *Can* she talk?"

"Yes, she can talk fine. Her lips didn't get burned as bad as other parts of her face."

"No offense, but that's deranged that you're having lunch with her and shit," said Louie. I bristled, even though, to be fair, I'd thought the same thing at various times. "Doesn't her face make you want to puke?"

"Nope."

Louie grinned at Holly. "You should've seen him when we

peeked through her window! He just about pissed himself. Say what you said. Say it for her. It was funny as hell."

"I don't remember what it was."

Louie recoiled. "*What the fuck is that?*" he said, in what I hope was a poor impression of me.

"Yeah, okay, I remember now. The thing is, that was really uncool of me. I was mortified by my behavior the next morning. That's why I went over to apologize, and that's how I discovered that she's a great person. She's the opposite of people who get drunk and peep into stranger's windows after dark. So I'm going to propose that we drop the comments that we wouldn't say to her face, and get this game started."

Louie chuckled. "To her face. That's funny."

"No, it wasn't. That wasn't intentional or clever."

"Are you really defending that freak?" asked Holly.

Now, as a reasonably intelligent, reasonably perceptive adult, I knew exactly what was happening here. Holly was well aware that I was not going to try to kick her ass. She was bored in a small town on a Sunday afternoon, and knew that if I reacted poorly to her comment, Louie would have to defend her honor. She simply saw the opportunity to watch her fiancé kick somebody's ass and seized it.

Therefore, the proper response should have been to chuckle, shake my head, and walk out of Doug's Booze Wasteland, leaving Louie and Holly to play another game of pool so as not to waste my fifty cents, after which they'd perhaps return home for some joyless sex.

On the flip side, at least I didn't smack the pool cue into Holly's face. That would have been incredibly inappropriate. I didn't smack it into Louie's face, either. I completely held my temper. All I did was, in a very even tone of voice, say, "Please don't call her a freak."

Holly glanced over at Louie. "Are you going to let him talk to me like that?"

Louie looked a bit surprised, since my request hadn't been the slightest bit rude. Then I think he immediately got where this was supposed to be headed, because he stood up straight, puffed out his chest, and said, "I'd like you to apologize to my fiancé."

I don't know. It's hard for me to get behind the idea that I should have apologized just to diffuse the situation. Sometimes you have to say "I'm sorry" for something that requires no apology, and sometimes, as I did, you have to say, "Go fuck yourself."

Louie blinked. "Did you mean me or her?"

"Take your pick."

"Are you going to let him talk to me like that?" Holly said for the second time in two sentences.

"I'm not sure he was talking to you."

"We'll say that I was talking to you," I told Louie.

"Okay."

"Are you going to let him talk to *you* like that?" asked Holly.

"I don't actually care how he talks to me."

"Well, I do. He's putting his dick in a freak and you're going to let him talk to us like that?"

"Are you going to let her talk to me like that?" I asked Louie. At that moment, I was too pissed off to be aware of the escalating absurdity of the conversation.

"Honestly, that was a little uncalled for," Louie told Holly. "You should probably apologize."

Holly gaped at him. "Are you kidding me?"

"No." Louie quickly realized that this was the incorrect answer. "I mean, yes. I mean, we should all apologize to each other. You haven't even broke yet and this game of pool is getting out of hand."

"I'll find something else to do," I said, turning around.

"Hey!" said Louie.

"What?"

"You didn't apologize."

"Let's just part ways."

"You owe my girlfriend—"

"Fiancé," Holly corrected.

"I know that."

"You said girlfriend."

"Yeah, but I know what you are."

"Then say it right."

"You owe my fiancé an apology," Louie notified me.

"Are we really going to do this?" I asked. "Are we really going to get into a bar fight? We're better than this."

"Then apologize."

Sometimes you have to say "Go fuck yourself," and sometimes, as I did, you have to say "I'm sorry" for something that requires no apology.

"I'm sorry." There. Done. I could get back to worrying about how Rachel's talk with her father was going.

"I don't think he meant it," said Holly.

"Obviously he didn't mean it," said Louie. "I wouldn't expect him to mean it. I just wanted him to do it."

"I totally meant it," I said. "That was the most sincere apology ever to pass through a human mouth. Now, if you'll so kindly excuse me, I've got to be going."

"He must be in a hurry to put his dick back in the freak," said Holly, who obviously figured that since this line had worked so well last time, it was worth a reprise. Holly was all about the greatest hits.

I wanted to ask her a second time to apologize for calling Rachel a freak, but we were trapped in the conversation from hell, and unless somebody broke through to the exit, we could be imprisoned in an endless loop forever.

"You two have a happy life together," I said. Of course, my own contribution to our shared misery was my need to get in the last word. There was no reason to say "You two have a happy life together" instead of just walking away. But I am a flawed human being and I accept that.

"I've never had sex with a crispy chick," said Louie. "You think she just flakes off onto the sheets? That's nasty."

Holly looked at Louie as if he'd gone too far. Louie looked back at her as if to say, "*I thought this was what you wanted!*"

I raised my fist.

"Oh, here we go!" said Louie, raising both of his fists.

"Kick his ass!" said Holly. I secretly hoped that she'd switched allegiances after the distasteful flaking comment and was speaking to me, but, no, she was still rooting for Louie.

"Wait, I can't fight you," I said, lowering my fist. "I'm a cartoonist. I can't risk hurting my hands."

"You joking?" asked Louie.

"No. It's how I make my living."

"Oh. Yeah, I guess that makes sense. You don't see surgeons going around getting into fights, either." He lowered his fists.

"You're going to let him get away with that weak excuse?" Holly asked.

"I like the guy," said Louie. "We had a good time. We had some drinks, we went out for a walk, Erik and I showed him Blister...it was fun. I wish you'd been there."

"I can't believe I'm marrying a coward."

Louie put his fists back in the air.

I sighed and put mine back in the air as well.

"Hey!" shouted Doug from behind the bar. "You want to fight, you take it someplace else!"

Louie and I lowered our fists.

"I don't feel like going someplace else," Louie muttered.

I decided that perhaps it was time for me to evolve into somebody who didn't need to get in the last word. So I turned and headed for the exit.

"So, are you leaving?" Louie called after me. "Or are we supposed to fight outside?"

I ignored him.

"I'll just assume that you're leaving," Louie called out as I reached the door. Without looking back, I gave him a thumbs-up.

I walked outside. Technically, this had achieved the desired purpose of distracting me from my thoughts for a while, and I hadn't injured my delicate hands, so all was well.

Except that Allen was standing next to my car.

Suddenly I was right back to white-hot rage.

"What the hell are you doing here?" I asked, walking toward him, fully prepared to break his nose.

"This isn't private property."

"I am *done* with you," I said. "Whatever fixation you've got on me is *over*, do you understand? I've already told the sheriff about your little stalking game."

He didn't move. I reached him and shoved him away from the car. I didn't care if I couldn't draw for a few months—it would be worth it to shatter my knuckles against his chin.

"I'm tired of this," I said. "Just go away. What's the matter with you?"

He reached into his inside jacket pocket, and I had about a second and a half to wish I'd been more cautious. Then he was pointing a gun at my stomach.

"Get in my truck," he said.

CHAPTER SIXTEEN

I did not want to get into his truck.

But Doug's Booze Wasteland wasn't exactly a high traffic area. I couldn't count on delaying Allen long enough for somebody else to walk out of the building, or a car to drive by. And I wasn't even sure that this would make him put his gun away—he might just shoot me and run.

I opened my mouth to say something, and couldn't think of a single thing, not even *"Please don't."*

Allen took a couple of steps forward, closing the gap from when I'd shoved him, and pressed the barrel of the gun against my stomach. "I'll do it," he said.

I looked into his eyes, and yeah, he would put a bullet in my gut, no question. Even if I found my voice, I wasn't going to waste his time by suggesting that he wouldn't really make good on his threat.

There was only one truck in the parking lot, and it was right next to my car. Not a lot of opportunity for a daring escape. For the immediate future, I was going to do whatever Allen wanted.

"Open the passenger door and get in," Allen told me.

I nodded. Moving slowly, but not too slowly, I walked over to his truck, carefully opened the door, and got inside. The interior of the truck was immaculate; nothing I could pick up to use as a weapon.

Allen climbed in on the driver's side. He pointed the gun at me. "Close the door and fasten your seatbelt."

I did both of those things without a word.

Allen closed the door and fastened his own seatbelt. I tried to figure out my odds of success if I were to suddenly lunge at him and try to wrestle the weapon out of his grasp. I decided that they were almost non-existent. Until I became certain that his plan was to execute me, I'd just play it cool and hope that we could reason this out.

He started the engine.

"Where are we going?" I asked.

"Don't worry about it."

"I'm sorry I didn't listen to you before," I said. "I didn't realize how strongly you felt about the matter." That sounded kind of sarcastic, which was not my intent. I was probably better off being too frightened to speak.

Allen drove out of the parking lot and down the dirt road. It was broad daylight and he didn't seem to care if anybody saw me in his truck. I wasn't sure if that was a good sign, or a really, really bad one.

"I told you to go," he said. "You knew you were supposed to leave and you didn't. This isn't my fault. This is your fault. This is completely your fault."

"I know," I told him, hoping to hell that playing along with him was the right way to go. "I screwed up, okay? It won't happen again."

"It sure won't."

"Are you going to kill me?"

Allen said nothing.

"Are you?" I asked. "I think it's a fair question."

"No," said Allen. "I'm not going to kill you."

Did this mean he was going to drop me off at the edge of town and sternly tell me not to return? I hoped so. That would be awesome.

"Then what are you going to do?" I asked.

"Don't ask any more questions."

We drove in silence for a few minutes. A couple of cars passed us going the opposite direction, but Allen didn't order me to duck out of sight. I wanted to believe that Allen simply thought he was within his rights to drive me out of town at gunpoint without legal ramifications.

He turned onto a narrower dirt road without a street sign.

"Why did you have to mess things up for everybody?" he asked. "Things were fine. Everybody had moved on. Why restart it all? None of this is any of your business. Why not leave things the way they were?"

"Things weren't okay for Rachel," I said.

"She was fine. She was getting better than she deserved."

"Why? Because she's unpleasant to look at?" *Don't argue with the crazy guy*, I warned myself.

"You think she's such a great person, this ray of sunshine that brings joy to the world, but she's not. She's a liar. A lying, selfish bitch."

"What makes you say that?"

"Look what she did to Brandon!"

"Maybe I'm missing part of the story," I admitted.

"Maybe you are."

"So fill me in. What did she do to him?"

"They'd talked about what they were going to do on her

eighteenth birthday! They'd planned it! She teases him for weeks, and then she's in this dress that shows off half her tits, and they drive out to the spot where they'd decided to do it, and then she goes, 'Ha ha, just kidding!' I'm not saying that girls have to put out, but they'd *planned* it! They'd *discussed* it! She told him to bring a condom!"

Allen was so angry that spit was flying from his mouth and hitting the steering wheel. I didn't think that pitching the idea of "no means no" was going to work with him.

"So may I debate your point?" I asked.

"I guess."

"The way I heard it, Brandon was being a complete jerk. Rachel may have said they were going to have sex, but if he was being obnoxious and disrespectful, it's his fault. He had his chance and he screwed it up. That's on him."

"The clown necklace was a harmless joke."

"Maybe, but when you're trying to get laid, sometimes a harmless joke isn't the right play. Look, I was eighteen, and I totally understand the raging hormones, but you're blaming the wrong person."

Allen shook his head. "No, I'm not."

"Allen, he slashed up her face with a straight razor. He burned her with a blowtorch. Are you really saying that she deserved it? There is no level of blue balls where what he did was right."

"I'm not saying she deserved everything. But she ruined his life."

"How long were you and Brandon friends?"

"Since second grade."

"So you'd been best friends for about ten years. I completely understand why you'd take his side. People do god-awful things sometimes, and that doesn't mean their family and friends abandon them. I admire your devotion to Brandon, I really do."

"He had big plans," said Allen. "He was going to get out of this shithole town. He would've taken her, too. Would've married her. Right now they'd be rich and happy and have two or three kids and she destroyed that life they could have had."

"We're starting to veer back into blaming the victim."

"I'll never stop blaming her."

"Then I'll quit trying to change your mind. You've said your piece, I've said mine, and I think we understand each other a little better now. So how about you stop the truck, let me out, and we'll go our separate ways?"

"I'll never see you around here again?" Allen asked.

"Never."

"I don't mean a year from now. I mean never."

"You will never lay eyes on me again."

"And you won't call the sheriff on me?"

"That's right."

"Then what I'm hearing from you, right now, at this moment, is that you think I'm stupid."

"No," I said. "I just want to go home and pretend this never happened. I want to put this whole trip behind me. It was all a mistake. You're right, none of this is my business."

"You're saying what you think I want to hear."

"I'm not saying that I want to leave. I'm saying that you've convinced me that it's in my best interest to leave. The gun and kidnapping thing worked. A job well done. You put enough of a scare into me that I don't want anything more to do with this place. Stop the truck, let me out, and it's over."

Allen did not stop the truck.

"It would be nice if it were that easy, wouldn't it?" he asked.

"Why can't it be?"

"As soon as you brought her out there, reminded everybody about her, you unburied shit that's not going to go back in the grave. If you had listened to me the first time, if you'd just left, things would've been okay, but I know damn well that you're only promising not to tell anybody because I've got a gun pointed at you. As soon as you're safe, you'll tell."

"How can I convince you that I won't?"

"You can't."

"Then we're at an impasse."

"No, we're not. You're acting like I care what promises you make. I don't. Your fate is already sealed, Jason Tray, and let me tell you, you are *fucked*."

"And now I don't believe you," I said. "There's no reason we can't talk this out. It's ridiculous to let it go any further."

"Is it? How about I raise the stakes? I burned down your cabin. I was smart about it, but if they do a thorough investigation I'm sure they'll figure out that it was done on purpose. See what I just did? I confessed to a crime. If I let you go, you'll tell somebody. Don't pretend you won't."

Was this the right time to go for his gun? Or unfasten my seatbelt, fling open the door, and hope that I was able to jump out of the truck without getting shot?

I gave myself maybe a one in a hundred chance of getting the gun away from him before he pulled the trigger, and that might've been optimistic. I wasn't quite there yet. Maybe if he hit a bump...

"You said you weren't going to kill me."

"That's right."

"So..."

"So either I'm lying my ass off, or I have other plans."

As the road curved to the left, I saw where it ended: in front of a small cabin. It was a rickety looking, unpainted piece of crap that didn't even look like it would meet the quality standards of a meth den.

"Did Blister tell you where it happened?" he asked.

"She said it was in a cabin."

"Did she say which one?"

"No."

"But I bet you've figured it out now, huh?"

Allen stopped in front of the cabin. He put the truck into park and turned off the engine.

"Brandon's family owned this cabin. We used to come out here and read *Playboy*. That was when we were maybe twelve or thirteen. I'd forgotten that we'd hidden them under the floorboards, but the cops found a bunch of them when they investigated the crime scene. Would've been embarrassing, except that everybody was focused on other stuff, obviously. The cabin doesn't get a lot of use these days. You can understand why Brandon's mom and dad don't want to be here, and the cabin where a girl was mutilated is a tough sell for a realtor, so they just kind of let it rot. I come here sometimes to think." He unfastened his seatbelt, keeping the gun pointed at me.

"Allen, what are we doing here?" I asked.

"You *should* keep asking questions. You really should, because I said I'd shoot you if you asked questions, and getting shot is way better than what's going to happen to you. So ask away. What do you want to know? Ask me anything."

I was silent.

"Get out of the truck," Allen told me.

He got out at the same time. If I sprinted and made it to the woods, I might be able to escape, but I'd have to run about a hundred feet to make it to something resembling cover.

Was Allen a good shot or a bad shot?

He struck me as somebody who enjoyed hunting.

Shit. I didn't want to die, and I most assuredly didn't want to get shot in the leg and dragged inside for whatever nightmare he had planned. What the hell was I going to do?

By the time I decided it was too risky to flee, it was too late anyway. Allen was right next to me.

"Walk over to the door," he told me.

I walked over to it. Maybe one of the drivers who'd passed us had been suspicious. Maybe Sheriff Baker was on his way at this very moment, and if I could keep Allen occupied for a few extra minutes, he'd arrive and save my ass.

Yeah, right. Nobody was going to save me.

I suddenly realized that I was very close to dropping to my knees and begging for mercy. I desperately hoped I could keep myself from doing that. I didn't want to go out that way. I wanted to keep my dignity.

Why hadn't I taken him more seriously? Why hadn't I gone back inside the bar and called the sheriff?

I stood in front of the door. There was a pretty big gap between two of the boards, but it was too dark inside for me to see anything.

"Don't open it quite yet," said Allen. "First, I'm going to raise the stakes again. I've got a story to tell."

CHAPTER SEVENTEEN

Brandon is sobbing. "I can't believe I did it."

He's said this over and over, at least ten times now. Allen isn't good at consoling people in their time of need, and he can't figure out what he should be doing to help.

"It'll be okay," he says.

"No, it won't! Aren't you even listening to me?" He wipes his nose on the sleeve of his suit. "I'm gonna go to jail."

"We won't let that happen," Allen assures him.

"I just...I just lost control of myself. Like somebody else took over my body. It was like I wasn't even there when it happened."

"At least you know you didn't get her pregnant," says Allen, in a failed attempt to lighten the mood. Up until a few weeks ago, when she'd dumped him for a football player, Allen had been screwing Sara Black every Tuesday and Thursday night, when her mom worked the late shift. It was great fun, but he'd lost a lot of sleep thinking about the possibility that he might accidentally knock her up.

This was supposed to be an incredible night for his buddy.

There were plenty of other girls at school who would've spread their legs for Brandon, or at least blown him, but no, Mr. Lame-Ass Romantic had to be with a prude like Rachel. They'd been together for over a year. A year! And she backed out on him?

What did she *think* he was going to do?

Of course he smacked her head against the dashboard.

Allen would've done a lot worse.

A *lot* worse.

"What am I going to do when she wakes up?" asks Brandon. "What am I going to say? I should take her to the hospital."

"Don't do that," says Allen. "It's just a bump on the head. She'll be okay."

"What if she has a concussion?"

"She doesn't."

"You don't know that! I knocked her unconscious!" Brandon buries his face in his hands and sobs like a goddamn baby. Allen hates Rachel for turning his best friend into this pathetic, sniveling wreck.

What was her problem? The clown jewelry was *funny*. It had been Allen's idea. They'd had an even funnier idea for later, but Brandon had called it off because he thought Rachel might be too mad.

Brandon stands up. "I'm taking her to the hospital."

"That's a bad idea."

"She could be hurt."

"What do you think her dad will do to you when he finds out?"

Brandon looks physically ill. "He's going to find out, no matter what. What if she's got internal bleeding in her brain or something, and he finds out I didn't take her straight to the emergency room?"

"No. Brandon, no." Allen stands up as well. "Rachel needs to understand that you weren't in your right mind. It's her fault. If she talks to a nurse, or her dad, or anybody else, they'll completely turn her against you. Even if she wants to forgive you, they won't let her."

Brandon nods. "You're right, they won't," he says. "What am I gonna do? She'll probably lose it when she wakes up and sees me. She won't talk to me. I know she won't talk to me. Why would she? I fucking hurt her. I never thought I would do something like that. It all happened in that one second. Just one second."

"Calm down."

"I can't!"

"I mean it."

"I'm going to jail!"

"Will you stop it?" Allen considers slapping his friend across the face, but decides against it. "Rachel likes me, right?"

"Yes."

"So I'll talk to her. If you leave, then maybe I can talk to her without her getting all emotional, and I can convince her that she should keep quiet about what happened."

"You want me to go home?"

"No. Go someplace where you won't have to talk to anybody. Just someplace where you can chill out and compose yourself."

"I don't know."

"If you don't like the idea, I'm not going to force you. I'm not the one who's looking at prison time for assault. But I'm the only person who will be on your side, so I'm the only person who can convince her to do the right thing."

"Yeah." Brandon sniffles and then wipes his nose on his sleeve again. "Yeah, I think that's what we should do. You talk to her. It's just what you said—she likes you. You two are friends, right? I consider you two friends. She might listen to you."

"We'll move her to my car," says Allen. "I can't lie to you, though. If she asks me to take her to the hospital, I'm going to, no questions asked. I can't become an accessory."

"Yeah, yeah, that's okay, I get that." Brandon nods rapidly, jiggling a line of snot that's dangling from his nose. "That might work. It really might work."

Together they put Rachel in the front seat of Allen's car. There's a pretty awful red bump on her forehead that will have to be explained, but she can say she bonked her head getting into the car. Allen has seen her be clumsy before.

Brandon throws his arms around Allen. "Thank you so much," he says. Allen doesn't like to be hugged, even by women, but he tolerates it.

"Go," he says. "Get out of here. I'll call you when I know what's going on."

"How will you call me? I won't be home."

"Just go, all right? She could wake up any minute."

Brandon gets in his car and drives away from the clearing in the woods where he was supposed to be getting laid for the first time. He should've left this place worrying about premature ejaculation, not prison time.

Allen gets into his own car and looks at Rachel. It's kind of concerning that she hasn't woken up yet. Maybe she won't wake up at all.

Maybe that would be better for Brandon.

Allen doesn't believe for one second that he can talk Rachel out of telling anybody. She's not the kind of girl who will say, "*Yes, my boyfriend physically assaulted me, but he was really horny, so I'll cut him some slack.*"

He doesn't know what kind of prison sentence this crime might carry. Maybe none at all. Maybe just community service. But it's certainly something that will destroy Brandon's future.

Rachel likes Allen, as far as he knows, but he's always hated her. Stuck-up bitch.

It won't be any great loss if she disappears.

It will be a great gain for Allen if she suffers. He's always wanted to do something like this.

When would he ever get this opportunity?

Never, right?

It was hard enough to find stray cats.

Brandon's cabin was only about ten minutes away. It would've been a nice, private place to screw Rachel, but she thought the cabin was disgusting...which, to be fair, it was.

Allen wouldn't screw her—he'd never screw his best friend's girlfriend, even if she was definitely an ex-girlfriend now—but he'd make good use of the privacy.

THE CLOWN SUIT FEELS PERFECT.

He wants to speak, wants to taunt her, but he also wants Rachel to die thinking that her agony is coming from somebody she loves.

Also, from a more practical standpoint, he can't guarantee that nobody will hear Rachel. If somebody shows up, he'll be glad his identity was hidden.

So many taunts.

So many things he wants to say to her as he slashes at her face, but he forces himself to remain silent and simply enjoy her reaction.

The razor looks so much better slicing across her face than it ever did with the cats. No fur to hide the wounds.

Most of her face is red. He'd love to cut her eyes, but if she's blind, she can't see the scary clown, and what fun is that?

Brandon is missing out.

He sets the razor aside and picks up the blowtorch. Oh, the cats *hated* the blowtorch. Rachel probably wouldn't be too keen on it, either.

Allen can't stop himself from giggling as he burns her flesh, but she can't hear him over the hiss of the blowtorch and the sound of her own muffled shrieks.

He hopes she doesn't choke on the rag he shoved into her mouth. He'd tested the rag on himself, seeing if he pack it in his mouth tightly enough that he couldn't get it out without using his hands. He could have just taped it, but there'd be less available surface area to burn.

Her face is totally ruined. It won't matter that she's unwilling to put out—nobody will want to have sex with her ever again.

What was that?

Allen turns off the blowtorch and walks over to the window. He thought he'd heard a car, but he doesn't see any headlights.

Now he's panicked. What the hell is he doing? How is he going to get away with this? How did he *ever* think he would get away with this?

I'm insane, he thinks. *I am really, truly, genuinely insane.*

He curses under the mask. He missed a couple of spots on Rachel's face, but the moment is over, the mood destroyed. He needs to slash open her throat and get out of here.

No. Wait. He doesn't need to kill her. He'll let Brandon take the blame. His subconscious mind had already worked it out. That's why Allen was wearing the costume in the first place.

It would be really shitty to do this to his friend, but things will never be the same between them anyway. Brandon made his own choice.

Yeah, he'd let Brandon take the fall. Brandon will tell everybody that Allen did it, of course, but if he leaves Rachel alive, her testimony will sink Brandon. Allen knows that he can hold up under interrogation, no problem.

He hurries out of the cabin. He takes off the clown costume and tosses it into the trunk of his car, along with the straight razor and blowtorch. Then he gets into his car and drives away.

Idiot! Idiot! Fucking idiot!

Allen cannot believe his own stupidity. His mind is so rattled that he's making mistake after mistake. He *deserves* to get caught.

He should have just tried to talk to her. Explain Brandon's side of the story. And if she did flip out, he should have taken her to the hospital so she could get her head checked out.

No, he shouldn't even have tried to talk to her. He should've taken her straight to the hospital. To hell with Brandon.

Instead, he'd transformed into a psychopath, and who knew how much evidence he'd left behind in the cabin? Yeah, he'd taken the weapons with him, and any footprints would've been left by the clown shoes that he was going to destroy, but what about the tire tracks? What if he'd lost an eyelash?

Allen holds his hand over his mouth, trying to keep from throwing up.

HE WALKS DEEP into the woods and buries everything.

He'll never do this again. It's not worth the anguish. He won't even kill another goddamn cat.

He goes home, sick and dizzy, waiting for the cops to show up.

They don't.

In fact, he never hears from Brandon again.

The son of a bitch ran away.

Allen keeps waiting for Brandon to contact him, or for somebody to realize that they made a mistake. But Rachel says it was Brandon, and since Brandon has disappeared, there's no reason for anybody to seek out alternate suspects.

Still, every day Allen checks the mail half-expecting to receive a letter that says, "*I Know It Was You!*"

None ever arrives, of course.

It takes several months for him to stop having nightmares, but then Rachel finally gets out of the hospital, and goes home to live with her father, and the nightmares start again.

Did he leave some clue? Will something click in her mind, making her realize that he was the one who turned her into a monster?

Five years after that night, he's almost able to forget about what he did.

And then, all of a sudden, Blister is no longer hiding away, and Allen thinks he's going to lose his mind.

CHAPTER EIGHTEEN

Allen sounded like he was becoming more and more unhinged as he told the story. He seemed to be simultaneously repulsed by his own words and ecstatic to be finally sharing the experience with somebody.

I didn't know what to say. It was bad enough when I thought he was just an angry gun-toting guy who wanted me to leave town. Now that I knew he was a full-fledged lunatic, I couldn't think of a way to reason with him. How could I explain that to somebody who'd mutilated an innocent girl that harming me would be a poor decision?

"Is it okay if I talk?" I asked.

"Sure."

"Now that I've heard your story, it's even more obvious that you're blaming the wrong person. How can you not blame Brandon? He's the one who put you in that situation, and then he ran away! He left you to clean up the mess yourself. None of this is Rachel's fault."

"I guess we'll have to agree to disagree. Open the door."

"I'll make you a deal. If you let me go, I'll leave town and I'll take Rachel with me. You'll never see either of us again."

"You're going to kidnap her?"

"No. She'd go willingly. I'm sure of it."

Allen narrowed his eyes. "Why would you be sure of that? What's happening between you two?"

This, ladies and gentlemen, was an example of saying the exact wrong thing. The madman holding you at gunpoint loathes Rachel? Tell him that you two are close enough that she'd run away with you! Well done, sir!

"It's not about me," I said, hoping he couldn't see the desperation on my face as I tried to come up with a new angle. "Rachel hates Lake Gladys. Hates everything about it. I mean, she spends her time in a shed, so why *wouldn't* she hate it? She asked me to bring her to Jacksonville, and I said no of course, because we barely know each other, and I figured she was just trying to use me to get out of here, but I can tell her I changed my mind. You won't have to worry about either one of us."

"Uh-uh," said Allen. "If I thought I could trust you, maybe that would work, but I know I can't."

"You can," I insisted. "You've made it very clear, crystal clear, that you're not someone to mess with. If I'd known that before, I never would have—"

"Shut up," Allen told me.

I decided to shut up. Babbling and begging was not going to save my life. I knew that the second he let me go, I'd be on my way to alert the authorities, and he knew that too, so there was no reason to continue to insult his intelligence by pretending otherwise.

"Open the door," he said.

I pulled open the door.

I'm not sure what I expected to see inside. Okay, that's not true:

144

I expected to see a complete horror show. But I didn't know whether it would be a "pile of severed heads in the corner" horror show, or an "intestines hanging from the ceiling like party banners" horror show, or a good old-fashioned "floors soaked with blood" horror show.

It was none of them. The cabin was mostly empty. There was a stained, torn, rat feces-covered mattress on the floor next to the far wall, and a wooden chair in the center. Some bungee cords were in a pile next to the chair.

There was also a small coffee table. Unlike everything else in the cabin, this had been recently dusted. Upon the table, propped up against a folded white cloth to display them more prominently, were a straight razor and a blowtorch.

I decided not to worry if I got shot. I spun around, hoping to grab Allen's arm and give it a really violent twist.

I'm pretty sure he was anticipating my reaction, because he punched me in the stomach with his free hand, and then when I doubled over, he bashed me on the back of the head with the gun. I fell to my knees.

I cringed, waiting for him to shoot me in the head, even though the razor and the blowtorch were a pretty clear indicator that he had far worse plans for me.

I reached for his foot, thinking that I might grab his ankle and yank him off-balance. Instead, he stomped on my hand. I howled with pain. He pushed down harder with his foot, grinding my fingers between the bottom of his shoe and the wooden floor.

Then he hurried over to the corner. There was a small cloth sack lying there that I hadn't noticed before.

I couldn't tell if any of my fingers were broken. They certainly felt like they were, but none of them were bent backwards and there were no protruding bones.

This was, presumably, my opportunity to get the hell out of

there, but after a punch to the stomach and blow to the skull I wasn't feeling particularly mobile.

Allen set down the gun and quickly picked up a small clear bottle and unscrewed the lid. He poured some liquid from the bottle onto a rag as he rushed back to me. I tried to fend him off, but he got the rag over my nose and mouth.

I didn't know what chloroform smelled like, if anything, but this wasn't it. This smelled like nail polish remover, which Allen must have decided would work just as well.

He may have been right. My nostrils burned and I couldn't breathe. I tried to cough but he had the rag pressed too tightly against my mouth. My eyes watered. He splashed some more liquid onto the rag, and I thought I was going to choke to death.

Finally he removed the rag.

I tried to crawl away, but I couldn't get my bearings. Everything was a blur. I was gasping for breath and then coughing and thinking about how I needed to force myself to stand up and run but I couldn't even manage to crawl.

Allen clubbed me again with the gun.

I remained conscious but useless. He grabbed me by my injured hand and dragged me across the floor. I struggled, somewhat, though not in such a way that it prevented Allen from getting me over to the chair.

He gave my hand an extra squeeze, then lifted me into the chair. This would have been a prime opportunity to elbow him in the ribs, or turn around and try to take a bite out of his throat, but instead I just sort of flopped around.

As I blinked away tears, he shoved the wet rag back into my face. If Allen wasn't careful, he *was* going to kill me before he got to disfigure me.

I got in a weak punch, but it didn't stop him from strapping three bungee cords around my chest. My chance to run away was gone. I was tied to a chair. In a cabin. By a maniac.

"*Don't*," I said.

Allen was not persuaded by the poetry of my speech. It took a couple of punches to get the job done, but soon Allen had strapped my arms and legs to the chair as well. He also put a gag in my mouth, though thankfully it wasn't soaked in nail polish remover. Apparently his extra planning time allowed him to do better than just stuffing a rag all the way into my mouth.

He knelt down in front of me. "We're in no rush," he said. "I'm going to step outside for a few minutes to give both of us a chance to calm down and catch our breath. I'll be right there, so if you try to get away, I'll hear you."

I wasn't sure exactly what punishment was implied by this warning. Was he going to do something even worse?

Allen stood up, walked toward the door, then stopped and turned back around to face me. He looked like he wanted to punch himself. He squeezed his eyes shut for a few seconds, then opened them again.

"I can't do that. I can't leave you alone in here. Not even if you're tied up and I'm right outside."

It wouldn't have mattered to me—I had no plan for escape.

Instead, Allen walked over to the mattress, brushed off a clean spot, and sat down on it. Then he just stared at me.

This wasn't calming me down.

So what was my escape strategy, if I worked under the assumption that I couldn't talk Allen out of this? These bungee cords were painfully tight. Even if I was able to discreetly scoot the chair a bit, it was right there in the center of the room, and it wasn't as if there was a giant nail jutting from the wall that I could use to cut the cord.

For the next few minutes I reviewed my available options, and I came up with the following plan: hope that somebody showed up to rescue me.

Or, if that failed, die of a heart attack before the really nasty stuff began. I felt like I was on the verge of cardiac arrest anyway. Honestly, I was proud of myself for not simply slipping into a catatonic state.

"Are you ready?" Allen finally asked.

I shook my head.

He stood up. "This is going to be horrible for you," he said. "While I'm doing it, I want you to remember that you brought this on yourself. You had a way out."

He walked over to the coffee table, and pointed his index finger back and forth between the straight razor and the blowtorch, as if trying to decide which one to select. It looked like something he'd practiced in the mirror, right down to the quizzical facial expression.

Then he picked up the razor.

"I couldn't talk when I did this to Blister, and it stole a lot of the fun away," he said. "But now I can talk all I want. And nobody is going to come looking for you here, so I can bide my time. I can watch you sweat. Watch you squirm. Are you thinking about how it's going to feel when I cut your face open, or are you already thinking ahead and worrying about the blowtorch?"

He walked over to me, slowly. Too slowly. It was almost comical. He was trying way too hard to be menacing. I'm not suggesting for an instant that he wasn't being successful at it, but if I were an uninvolved spectator, I'd be laughing at his effort.

"You like Blister, huh? Think she's fun? Think she's neat? Maybe you should be more like her. What do you think about that? Maybe you should be more like the person you admire so very much." He held the razor up to my cheek and pretended to consider what to do next. "Wait a minute...I've got it! Maybe you should *look* like her."

Allen said this as if it were a great big shock, even though I'd figured out where this was headed long ago. I wished I weren't the one about to be mutilated, so I could scoff at his technique.

He placed the corner of the blade against my right temple.

Muffled by the gag, I begged him not to do this.

Allen grinned and very slowly slid the blade down the side of my face. It wasn't that deep of a cut, as far as I could tell, but it definitely hurt and I could feel the blood trickling down my cheek.

He cut all the way to the bottom of my jaw.

He held up the bloody blade for my inspection, then licked it. That is, he pretended to lick it. I'm not sure if he didn't want to taste the blood or if he didn't want to cut his tongue, but either way, he didn't *quite* lick the blade.

Again, it would've been amusing if I didn't have blood running down my face.

"Another cut?" he asked.

I vigorously shook my head.

"I agree. Let's mix it up. When I did Blister, it was cut, cut, cut, burn, burn, burn, but it's more interesting to go back and forth, don't you think?"

He placed the razor back on the coffee table, then picked up the blowtorch.

I screamed and struggled against the cords, but it wasn't doing a bit of good. If Allen wanted to mangle and burn me beyond recognition, that's what was going to happen.

He held the blowtorch up to me. "Maybe you'll luck out," he said. "Maybe it won't have any fuel. Maybe I didn't bother to make sure it was in working order before I dragged you all the way out here."

Allen turned it on. He looked at the small blue flame and

smiled. "Oh well. At least you had those few seconds to fantasize about a better outcome, right?"

I'm not ashamed to admit that, by now, I was crying. Not a stoic single tear, but terrified, panicked, *please God don't let this happen to me* sobbing. I wasn't sure how Rachel had made it through this experience with her sanity intact, and I hadn't even felt any of the true agony yet.

He held the flame up to my eye for several seconds.

"Nope," he said, lowering it. "I wouldn't want to burn out your eyeball. Then you'd only have one eye left to watch me with. I wouldn't want you to miss anything."

He slapped me in the face, on the side that he'd cut. "Stop thrashing around so much. You can move around all you want after I send you back out into the world, but while you're in my chair, stop moving."

I stopped moving.

Allen wiped up some blood with his thumb. "Sorry to have aggravated your wound. You know, when Rachel was in your situation, I thought of this thing where I wanted to tell her how considerate I was, because I was going to cauterize her wounds for her. Just a special little service I could offer. I'm really excited that I finally get to use this line, five years later. So, Jason Tray, because I am a friendly and considerate host, I am going to cauterize your wound, free of charge."

He placed his free hand tightly over my neck to hold my head in place. Then he held the blowtorch up to the top end of the cut and pressed the flame to my skin.

I'd been burned before, of course, but it was always: touch hot stove, recoil, apply ice. Sustained burning was simply not something I'd ever experienced. Though I wasn't a strong believer in the afterlife, I could suddenly understand why the fear of an eternity of hellfire influenced some people's daily choices.

I'm sure there was worse pain in the world, but at the moment I couldn't think of anything more unbearable than what I was experiencing right then.

Allen giggled as he moved the flame down the entire length of my cut.

CHAPTER NINETEEN

When he finished cauterizing the wound, Allen turned off the blowtorch.

He was no longer giggling, or even smiling.

He stepped away, and let the blowtorch fall to the floor.

"This isn't how it was supposed to be," he said, almost pouting. "This isn't fun. There's nothing fun about this. Shit!" He kicked the blowtorch. It spun across the floor and struck the wall.

I should've felt relieved, but the pain blinded me to any other emotion.

Allen began to pace. "It's not fair. This isn't working right. Why didn't you just leave? I asked you to leave. Why didn't you do it? Now look at us! Look at what you did to us!"

He walked over to the cabin door, and now I could focus enough to hope that he might walk out and leave me here. Instead, he stared at the door for a moment, fist clenched, as if considering punching it in frustration. I hoped he did and shattered his hand.

He didn't. He continued pacing.

"Why couldn't this have worked out? Why can't anything ever

go right for me? Why does everything get fucked up every single fucking time?"

I had no answer for that, and not merely because I was gagged.

Allen sat down on the mattress. For a moment I thought he was actually weeping, but he didn't go quite that far.

Was he going to simply quit torturing me? That level of good fortune seemed unimaginable. Raging psychopaths didn't just wuss out, did they?

I tried to spit out the gag, because maybe this would be my actual opportunity to talk some sense into him, but it was on too tight.

Now Allen was whispering something to himself. I couldn't tell what he was saying, but it didn't sound motivational.

He began to chew on the end of his index finger. Not just the nail, the actual finger.

He stood up, took a couple of steps toward me, then changed his mind and sat back down on the mattress.

"Shit!" he said.

Allen closed his eyes and took several deep breaths, as if he were trying to psyche himself up. Finally, he opened them again and looked over at me.

He let out a sheepish laugh.

"What the hell was that, huh?" he asked. "That is seriously humiliating. I don't know what happened. I just lost it there for a minute."

He stood up.

"It won't happen again," he assured me.

My panic returned in full force as Allen went over and retrieved the straight razor.

"Do you know what Blister has that you shouldn't have?" he asked. "A nose. We'll fix that." It was another line that sounded rehearsed, but that didn't make it any less frightening.

He walked over to me, waving the razor back and forth in a menacing manner but still looking completely freaked out. If he hadn't planned out his sinister dialogue beforehand, I doubt he would have been able to say anything clever.

I didn't want to lose my nose. I really, truly, wholeheartedly did not want to lose my nose.

Allen stood in front of me. He feinted a swing at my ear, forced a smile, then leaned his face down right next to mine.

"Is there one last thing you'd like to smell before I do the deed?" he asked.

There were probably a lot of amusing answers I could have given him, but I wasn't in the right mindset for quipping. I did realize that in Allen's anguish, he'd made one pretty big mistake.

He'd left himself open to a head butt.

In action movies, there's an interesting biological phenomenon that when two heads collide, the party who initiated the head butt is immune to the effects of two skulls crashing together. This was not an action movie. To counter the damage to my own cranium, I had to aim for a softer target.

Allen shouldn't have threatened my nose.

My forehead smashed into his face, and the *crack* was as satisfying as the sound of popping open a can of beer on a hot summer day. Allen howled and stumbled away, hands over his nose, blood already spurting between his fingers as the razor clattered on the floor.

I jerked myself to the right, tipping over the chair. I didn't need it to completely break apart—I just needed to damage it enough to loosen the cords.

I struck the floor, hard.

As far as I could tell, all I'd done was cause the right arm of the chair to swivel a bit. I tugged my arm as hard as I could, and it began to slide free.

Allen was on his knees, wailing.

I pulled my right arm free, and then reached over and frantically worked on the cords binding the left.

Blood had run down Allen's face and neck, and was gushing onto the front of his shirt. I had *seriously* messed up his nose. Not as bad as slicing it off, but it would be several days before he stopped talking funny.

As I got my left arm free, Allen removed one hand from his nose. Did it hurt more to have your nose broken or to have the side of your face burned? I thought that the fire had to be worse, but Allen was reacting even more poorly to his injury than I had to mine.

He picked up the blowtorch.

I picked up the razor.

I started to saw through the cords that were binding my chest, but the razor wasn't doing a very good job. It would be easier to drop the razor and just reach behind me and unhook the cords by hand...except that right now I needed a weapon.

Allen turned on the blowtorch, spewing a constant stream of curses under his breath. It looked like some blood was getting into his mouth.

I lashed out with the razor. He was too far away for me to actually hit him; I just wanted to make it clear that he shouldn't come too close to me.

He watched me for a moment, and then apparently decided that since I was still mostly strapped to an overturned chair, the danger was minimal. He crouched down just out of range.

"I'll make you a deal," he said, though I could barely understand him. "Give that to me and I won't burn you to death."

I tugged down the gag. "Try to take it."

"I'll set your hair on fire."

"I'll still kill you," I said, with way more confidence than I felt, especially because if Allen took a moment to evaluate the entire situation, he'd remember that he had a perfectly good gun. Hopefully he remained committed to the idea of inflicting slow agony upon me.

Allen seemed unsure of how to proceed. Clearly, he still had the advantage, but I had two free hands and a weapon.

Would this be a good time to scream for help? Probably not. I wasn't sure if anybody would even hear me, and it was crucial that Allen not decide to simply cut his losses and murder me.

He stood back up. Walked backwards a few steps, not taking his eyes off me. I couldn't figure out what he was doing, until suddenly I realized that he was making room to get a running start. He was going to rush at me and kick me.

Shit.

He ran at me.

I was going to have to absorb the kick, and hope to get in a really vicious slash with the razor while he was there.

I assumed he was going to try to kick me in the head, possibly snapping my neck, or in the chest, possibly shattering a few ribs. Instead, he went for my hand, kicking at me as I swung at him. I aimed for his ankle. Missed. The blade struck the bottom of his shoe as he kicked it out of my hand.

The razor slid across the room, far out of my reach.

I grabbed Allen's other ankle with my free hand—which still hurt like hell from Allen stepping on it the last time I tried this trick, but apparently still worked—and yanked him off-balance. He fell backwards onto the floor, smacking his head. The blowtorch landed on his chest, but sadly, the flame had already gone out.

He didn't immediately move.

I quickly reached behind my back and began to unfasten the bungee cords. Allen was still conscious, but dazed, so if my hand continued to work and I didn't waste any time...

He groaned. He said something that I believe was an expression of how much he hated me, but I really couldn't understand enough of his words to say for sure.

The cords were there to keep me in place while he mutilated me; they weren't intended to be something inescapable if I were left alone. (At least I didn't think so. Allen was no criminal genius but he seemed smarter than that.) So I was able to unfasten them, one after the other, until my torso was free. From there, I could contort my body well enough to begin working on the cords that bound my legs.

Holy crap, I was going to get out of this alive and mostly unmangled!

Allen sat up. His nose was hideously swollen, and his face was covered in blood, tears, and a generous stream of mucus. He let out a scream of frustration and rage that made me think the poor son of a bitch had legitimately gone feral.

He turned the blowtorch back on and began to crawl toward me, leaving a black streak across the wooden floor as the flame dragged across it.

My legs were almost free.

Allen said something else. I literally could not understand a single word of it, nor could I figure anything out from context clues except that it was negative in tone.

He lunged at me with the blowtorch. I screamed in pain as the flame touched my shoulder, but fortunately my shirt hadn't—no, shit, my shirt *had* caught on fire.

I punched Allen square in the nose.

He didn't make a damn sound. Not a scream, not a gasp, not a grunt, nothing.

It was only a candle-sized flame on my shirt and I quickly patted it out. Then I unfastened the last couple of cords and, free at last, crawled toward the razor. The gun would have been a better choice, but Allen was between me and that most useful of weapons.

As I crawled, I realized that Allen was not the only one making poor decisions. The chair would've been a better weapon than the razor. Oh well. Too late now.

I picked up the razor and spun around. Allen had stood up yet again. The guy looked utterly pitiful, though not enough to make me feel sorry for him.

I stood up as well. He held up the blowtorch, and I held up the razor, as if we were going to have a damn swordfight.

He rushed at me, and I rushed at him, and, yes, our weapons connected as if we were pirates or knights, except really awful ones. We parried twice more, and then I slashed him across the lower arm, cutting deep.

He almost dropped the blowtorch. His hands were so slick with blood that I'm surprised he was able to hold onto it at all, but somehow he sustained his grip.

I lunged with the razor, jabbing him in the chest.

Allen bellowed with fury and then threw the blowtorch at me. I dodged enough that it bounced off my ear instead of striking me in the forehead, which still hurt like hell.

He pointed at me, eyes wide. When he shouted, this time I got his meaning: "*Blister's dead, you son of a bitch!*"

And with that, apparently he'd had enough of our little fight. Allen turned and ran. He threw open the cabin door and raced outside toward the truck.

I would've been delighted to see him go if he hadn't threatened Rachel. As he climbed into the truck, I ran over and picked up the gun that he really shouldn't have left behind.

He started the engine.

I took aim at his grotesquely swollen, bloody face.

I pulled the trigger. Nothing happened, because I'm not a gun expert and I'd left the safety on. I wasn't even immediately sure how to turn it off. I fumbled with the gun for a moment as Allen backed away from the cabin.

Fortunately, he either had to turn around, or make his escape in reverse. I took aim again, pulled the trigger, and this time the gun fired. It also recoiled far more than I'd expected. I hit the front windshield but missed Allen by a good two feet.

He sped off, apparently indeed planning to do this in reverse.

I lowered my aim. Better to shoot for the tires or the engine or something that would stop the truck. Anything in the lower half.

I fired, hitting the front left tire, which was not the tire I was aiming for, but I'd take it.

I fired again, missing completely.

My fourth shot also missed completely. The fifth shot, however, got the front right tire, which *was* the one I was aiming for.

The truck stopped.

Allen wasn't getting away in that thing. And, if this was a six-shooter (I wasn't sure) and had been fully loaded (I assumed it had been), I had one more shot to take him out.

He got out of the truck and ran for the woods.

I took very careful aim, trying to point the barrel at the center of his back.

I squeezed the trigger.

Missed.

Was it close? No idea. I couldn't tell what I'd hit, if anything, but no gout of blood spurted from Allen, and he hurried out of the clearing.

I squeezed the trigger again, hoping for bonus bullets, but no, this had been a six-shooter.

Dammit.

I kept myself fit, but still, I had the body of a cartoonist, and

Allen was fifteen years younger. In a race through the woods, he was going to win, even if he was gushing more blood than I was.

Was there a shortcut to Rachel's home through the woods? The dirt road had swerved quite a bit, so I had no idea if Allen was headed in the right general direction, but he'd walked out to the cabin a lot as a kid, so he'd know the area. That didn't mean he knew how to get to Rachel's place from here.

Instead of following him through the woods, my best bet was to run along the road. Once I got off the small dirt road and made it to the bigger dirt road, I might be able to flag down a car, and get there ahead of him.

Maybe Allen would change his mind. Or conveniently bleed out before he made it there.

I tossed the gun away. It wasn't any good to me without bullets, and a Good Samaritan would be more likely to pick me up if I weren't carrying a firearm.

Then I ran.

CHAPTER TWENTY

Though I got winded pretty quickly, I forced myself to push through it. I couldn't let Allen get to Rachel before me. Not that I'd do more good against the psychopath than Rachel herself; she would, most likely, simply blow his head off. I just needed to take away his element of surprise.

I flexed my hand as I ran. It was sore and swollen, and I didn't think I'd be drawing Zep the Beetle for at least a couple of weeks. As soon as it was healed, I'd draw a picture of Zep taking a dump on Allen's head. He could put it up on the wall of his prison cell.

I was scared to touch the side of my face, which still felt like it was burning. I'd have given anything for an ice pack. In a world where Rachel had received the same treatment times a hundred, I felt terrible worrying about the cosmetic aspect, but...I now had a giant scar running down the side of my face. I wondered how bad it looked. Probably not as awful as I was imagining.

If Rachel and I ended up together, I could tell her that I'd done it in an act of solidarity.

I was completely out of breath, but refused to stop, until gravity made the decision for me and I tripped. I slammed onto the ground and lay there for about half a minute, giving my lungs a chance to catch up with my sense of resolve. Then I got back up and resumed the run.

What if Allen had a really good shortcut? What if he'd taken Rachel by surprise, and right now was making the rest of her body match her face?

He wasn't. He didn't have the blowtorch anymore.

He still could be hurting her.

She still could be dead.

I made it to the wider dirt road about ten minutes after I left the cabin. I couldn't remember how far the nearest home had been. This whole area had seemed pretty desolate. There'd been several other small dirt roads along the way, but I wasn't sure if they led to anybody's houses or not.

Maybe Allen would run into a tree and completely splatter his face. In his current condition, he wouldn't have to hit the tree very hard.

I supposed he could have looped around and was following me, or was ready to leap out into the road in front of me. I wasn't really worried about that. Bring it on. I'd actually feel much better if he attacked me again. I'd leave him lying on the ground with a dozen broken bones, and he wouldn't get the chance to mess with Rachel.

Was that the sound of a car?

I stopped running for a second, unable to believe my good luck. The way things were going, I'd expected to have to run all the way to Rachel's before somebody picked me up.

Yes, it was a car! A beat-up gray sedan came into view, moving in the opposite direction that I was running. I moved into the middle of the road and waved my arms over my head, and the car stopped right in front of me.

I hurried over to the passenger-side door and threw it open. The driver, a girl who was probably about sixteen, looked at me in wide-eyed horror, and I realized that from her perspective a frantic-looking stranger with blood on his clothes and a fresh scar was inviting himself into her vehicle.

"I swear I'm not a killer," I said. "I need a ride really bad."

The girl looked like she desperately wanted to floor the accelerator and speed off, but feared that it was already too late.

I went ahead and got into the car. "I'm not going to hurt you."

"Do you need me to take you to the hospital?" she asked in a small, scared voice.

"Yes," I said, because it sounded more credible than, "*I need you to drive me to my girlfriend's house before a homicidal maniac gets to her.*"

I shut the door and she drove off, not going as quickly as I'd like.

"What happened to you?" she asked.

"A welding accident."

"Did you fall on your blowtorch?"

"Yeah."

"It looks like it hurts."

"It does."

I wasn't prepared to look at myself quite yet, but I couldn't stop myself from lowering the visor and glancing in the mirror. In truth, my crazed eyes were a little more disturbing than the wound...but it was a pretty goddamn awful wound. Nobody would be locking me in a shed, but until I got this patched up, I'd be scaring kids and teenaged girls.

"You should be more careful," the girl said.

"I will. Could you drive faster?"

"I just got my license."

"That's okay. I trust you not to crash."

"I don't trust myself. And it's my mom's car. I promised her I'd be careful."

"If you get in a wreck, I'll pay for the damages. Have you heard of the comic strip *Off Balance*?"

"No."

"I draw it. It's pretty successful. So you don't have to worry about the car."

"I don't want to hit somebody, though."

"You're right, I don't want you to hit somebody either."

She turned onto the paved road, and I realized that we were going to pass Doug's Booze Wasteland in about a minute.

"Change of plans," I said. "I'm going to have you drop me off at my car. After you do, I need you to call the sheriff. Tell them to send a car out to Malcolm Kramer's house. It's an emergency."

"Malcolm Kramer?"

"Yes."

"The one with the deformed daughter?"

"Yeah. Tell them to hurry."

"Did she break loose or something?"

"Yes, she's on a rampage."

"For real?"

"No. Pull in here."

She pulled into the parking lot, and I opened the door before she'd even come to a complete stop. "Thank you," I said, waiting until she'd come to a complete stop before I actually exited the vehicle.

I ran over to my car and got inside. Ignatz barked happily. "Hi, buddy," I said, starting the engine. "You would've bitten the crap out of him if you'd been there, wouldn't you? Good doggie."

I sped away from Doug's Booze Wasteland. I'd definitely make it to Rachel's before Allen got there. No way would he beat me. Not a chance. That loser was probably stuck in a bear trap right now, trying to gnaw off his own foot.

It would take about ten minutes to make it to Rachel's if I drove at a safe, legal speed, so I figured I could make it there in about six. I did slow down a bit before cruising through the red light.

Rachel would be fine. Perhaps she'd meet me with a great big grin and announce that Malcolm had given us his blessing.

I wished my face would stop hurting. I was probably doing serious damage to it by not putting ice or something on it, but obviously intercepting the psychopath going after Rachel had to take priority.

Does your face hurt? No. Well, it's killing me. Ha ha ha.

Was I losing it? Maybe a bit. But hey, right now I was only the *second* most insane person in Lake Gladys, so at least I had that going for me.

I didn't try to swerve around the squirrel that ran into the road. Fortunately for my squirrel karma, I missed it anyway.

When I finally pulled into Malcolm's driveway, he was sitting on the porch in his rocking chair, shotgun on his lap, looking pretty freaking mad.

He stood up as I got out of my car, but as he saw my condition his expression changed from anger to confusion. I hurried onto the porch.

"What the hell happened to you?" he asked.

"Has the sheriff called you?"

"No."

"Is Rachel inside?"

Malcolm shook his head. "We had a fight. She left."

"Left? Where'd she go?"

"No, I didn't mean 'left' left." He pointed to the shed. "She's in there, blasting her damn music." I could actually hear the music all the way up here. Apparently Rachel used hard rock to blow off steam after a family spat.

"She could be in serious danger."

"From who? What happened to your face?"

There wasn't time to give a full explanation of the wacky misunderstandings that had led to our current predicament, so I just blurted out: "Allen's the one who hurt Rachel!"

"What?"

"It was him. He was in a costume. He's the one who did that to Rachel's face, and he tried to do the same thing to me, and now he's on his way to hurt her again."

Malcolm gaped at me as if a giant erect penis had suddenly sprouted from my forehead.

"I know, it's a lot to take in," I said. "We need to get Rachel in here."

"I want you to pretend for a moment that I'm mentally retarded," said Malcolm. "What exactly are you saying?"

"You. Killed. The. Wrong. Guy."

Malcolm looked like he was going to puke.

"Don't get me wrong, Brandon was still a piece of shit," I said. "But he was mostly innocent. Allen, meanwhile, is acting like he's off every one of his meds."

"You stay here," Malcolm told me. "If you move, I'll shoot you."

I decided to take him at his word and didn't move as he walked off the porch and went over to Rachel's shed. He knocked on the door and said something that I couldn't hear. A moment later, he returned to the porch.

"She told me to go fuck myself, so that's good," he said. "Let's go inside."

"We can't! You have to bring her over here!"

"You can see her door and her window from inside. Unless he

breaks through her back wall, we'll see him." He pointed the shotgun at me. "Get inside."

I went inside and hurried into the kitchen so I could watch through the window. Malcolm followed, leaving his front door open, presumably in case we needed to rush out there to blow Allen away.

"How could I have known?" Malcolm asked. "Who else would it have been? It doesn't make any sense."

"I'm not here to point fingers," I said. "This isn't about what you did five years ago. This is about what's happening right now."

"I'll watch," said Malcolm. "There's an ice pack in the freezer."

I wanted to protest, but no, the ice pack was a good idea. I opened the freezer, searched for a moment, and didn't see one, so I just picked up a TV dinner and pressed it to my face.

"Does he have a gun?"

"No. When he ran off he didn't have anything. That doesn't mean he didn't stop somewhere."

"All right."

"Seriously, Malcolm, you can't worry about what happened to Brandon right now."

"It's easy for you to say that. You're not the one who killed him. Who will take care of Rachel if I go to jail?"

"I will. And you're not going to jail."

"The hell you will. We've got some ugly unfinished business. But we'll postpone."

"Yeah, it might be a good idea to save that shit for after your daughter's life is no longer in danger."

Malcolm ignored my sarcasm. "We can't have your car in the driveway. Two houses away, on the left, it's a red house—they aren't home. Park in their driveway."

"Are you kidding me?"

"Do you *think* I'm kidding? Get your car out of here and then get your ass back. I'll be watching you."

I didn't want to waste time arguing, and I definitely didn't want Malcolm to decide that he'd be better off just shooting me, so I hurried out of the house and back to my car.

I drove to the correct house. I hated to leave Ignatz behind, but he'd be in more danger if he was running around, and I was pretty sure that my little Schnauzer would not be the one to defeat Allen.

I parked my car in the empty driveway, then hurried back. I didn't even think about just driving away and getting the authorities myself, which surprised me, because it seemed like the kind of thing I'd at least want to consider as a viable option. I still wanted to handle this quietly, without Malcolm's colossal blunder being dragged into the spotlight.

Malcolm seemed a little bit shocked to see me return. Maybe this would earn me a point or two. We went back inside and into the kitchen. I traded out the TV dinner for a bag of frozen broccoli.

A car approached.

Malcolm left the kitchen and peered through the front window. "It's Baker," he said.

"Good."

"No, not good." Malcolm gestured at me with the barrel of the shotgun. "Hide in the bedroom."

"Why the hell would I hide?"

"Because I don't want him to know you're here, dipshit!"

"I get *that*, but why—?"

"In the bedroom. You make a single noise and we'll have problems."

I was ninety percent sure that Malcolm would not actually blow my chest open with a shotgun if I didn't hide silently in his bedroom, but it was that last ten percent that concerned me. "If you put her in danger, I'll never forgive you," I told him.

"I'm keeping her out of danger. Work with me here, and I'll work with you. Understand?"

Did he mean that he'd give Rachel and I his blessing if I didn't let the sheriff know that there was a homicidal maniac on the way? This was truly not a normal course of events. I decided to play along, went into Malcolm's bedroom, and closed the door most of the way.

I wasn't going to hide in the closet or under the bed or anything. If Sheriff Baker decided to take a look around, he'd find me, and I'd tell him everything.

"Good afternoon," I heard Malcolm say. "What's going on?"

"Well, I got kind of a disturbing call. Apparently a man who matches the description of Jason Tray told a young girl that it was vitally important that I show up here."

"What an asshole," said Malcolm.

"What makes you say that?"

"He's trying to go out with my daughter. I mean romantically."

"Ah."

"We had what you might call a spat, and I sent him away. I'm sure he's trying to get revenge."

"Did you threaten him?"

"I guess I might have."

Even though they were on the front porch, I could hear Sheriff Baker sigh. "Jesus, Malcolm, you can't do things like that. He seems like a perfectly decent gentleman. A bit old for Rachel, maybe, but there are...you know, extenuating circumstances. She's twenty-three years old. You can't control her boyfriends. You have to face the reality that she's not a little girl anymore, and you have to let her live an actual life. As far as I'm concerned, you owe Mr. Tray an apology, although I suppose that calling me was kind of a low move on his part."

"To be fair to him, Rachel and I had something of a screaming match ourselves. He was just worried, I suppose. When he comes back, yeah, I'll...I don't know, I'll talk to him. I'll let him see her, maybe. It's tough for me, you know?"

Wow. Malcolm was a skilled liar. I was kind of impressed.

"I know," said Baker. "It's hard enough when there isn't a history of crazed ex-boyfriends. Do you need me to hang around, make sure you hold your temper?"

"I'll be okay."

"I'd like to have a few words with Rachel before I head off, if you don't mind."

Malcolm chuckled. "Good luck with that."

A minute later, I pushed open the bedroom door and stepped out into the living room. Malcolm was in the kitchen, watching through the window. The music stopped, and I could see Rachel's door open and Baker walk inside her shed.

Malcolm looked back at me. "It went fine."

"I still don't understand why we don't want the sheriff here. I love the idea of having him here. I'd invite eight more like him if I could. He already knows what you did to Brandon, so why the secrecy?"

"As far as he knows, Brandon completely deserved what he got. It's all different now."

"But he was complicit in covering it up. He doesn't want this story to get out any more than you do."

"I disagree. I'm willing to kill again. I don't think he is."

"Aw, shit."

"Stop talking." Malcolm returned his attention to the window. Sheriff Baker stepped out and Malcolm waved for me to duck out of sight. He walked out onto the front porch.

"She's pretty mad at you," Sheriff Baker called out, sounding amused. Rachel's music was on again. "You've got some groveling to do, though I'd give it a couple of hours."

"Yeah, all right."

"If Mr. Tray's behavior turns into harassment, don't hesitate to give me a call. Otherwise, I think you need to sit back and let nature take its course. I looked him up. He's doing pretty well for himself. There are far worse men who could be in Rachel's life."

"I screwed up, I get it. I'll let you know if I win back my 'World's Greatest Father' mug."

I heard Sheriff Baker drive away.

"Now what?" I asked.

"Now we wait for that son of a bitch to show up."

A couple of minutes later, he did.

CHAPTER TWENTY-ONE

Allen stepped out of the woods next to the shed.

Was the timing coincidental, or had he been waiting for Sheriff Baker to leave?

I couldn't believe he'd actually shown up. Whatever criticisms you wanted to make about Allen, and there were many, he had balls. His nose was no longer spurting blood, but it didn't look like he'd bothered to wipe any of the old blood from his face. If I hadn't known it was him, I wouldn't even have recognized him.

I rushed out of the kitchen, expecting Malcolm to immediately follow. Instead, he slid open a drawer.

I gaped at him. "What are you waiting for?"

Malcolm took out a butcher knife.

"What the hell are you doing?" I asked. "We've got a shotgun!"

"Rachel will hear a gun," he whispered, as we walked through the kitchen and out onto the back porch. He scooped up the shotgun with his free hand. "I'll shoot him if we need to."

Holy freaking crap. How had a butcher knife entered the

equation? I wanted to protest, but Allen was standing six feet from Rachel's shed, staring at it, and we needed to *move.*

Malcolm pointed the knife at me. For a second I thought he was threatening me, but he was actually just signaling that I should step back inside. I reluctantly did so.

"He hasn't seen us yet," Malcolm whispered. He extended the shotgun to me, and I took it. "If things get out of control, kill him. But if they don't get out of control, wait for me to sneak up on him."

"If you're sneaking up on him with a butcher knife, things are already out of control."

"Use your judgment," he said. He peeked outside. Allen was still standing next to the shed, staring at a wall that had no door or window. Was he building up his courage?

This made absolutely no sense. We should rush right out there, make as much noise as possible, and scare him off. Why was I going along with this? Sure, I didn't have some long-buried secret from my past to worry about, but if I let him murder Allen in a manner that wasn't exactly self-defense, I'd have my own ghoulish little secret.

All Rachel and I had done was kiss. This was an overwhelming burden to accept just so her beloved father wouldn't suffer the consequences of his own mistake. I needed to turn the shotgun on Malcolm and explain that we were going to handle this my way.

Allen walked around the back of the shed.

"I'm going," said Malcolm. He ran off the porch, moving with rather shocking stealth (he'd seemed like more of a lumbering kind of fellow to me) toward the shed.

This was the worst idea ever. I was putting Rachel at risk to keep Malcolm out of trouble, and I didn't even particularly like the guy.

Well, no, Rachel wasn't really at risk, at least not at the

moment. Malcolm was right—if Allen wasn't on the side with the door or the window, he couldn't actually get in.

The only danger was that Rachel might come outside to investigate. But she wouldn't hear Allen walking around; hell, the way her music was blasting, she might not even hear the shotgun. Malcolm might as well have blown Allen away.

Malcolm made it all the way to the shed.

I couldn't stand around and wait in his house. If I ruined his plan, so be it, but no way was I letting Allen get anywhere close to Rachel's window.

I walked off the porch and headed toward the shed.

Not that I had any intention of murdering Allen. I wouldn't hesitate to pull the trigger if I had no choice, but I was perfectly content to hold Allen at gunpoint. Though he was insane, he was not, to the best of my knowledge, suicidal. If he had a shotgun pointed at him, he wouldn't give us any trouble.

Malcolm hurried around the back of the cabin.

A second later, as if we were in a wacky bedroom farce, Allen stepped around the other side.

If this had truly been a farce, he would have gone about his own business without noticing me. But this was real life, if you can call it that, and he saw me.

His mouth dropped open.

My presence can't have been that much of a surprise, since he knew I knew where he was headed. He may have been reacting to the shotgun.

I wanted to shout out to let him know not to try anything, but it suddenly occurred to me that this might draw out Rachel, if she heard it over her music. I decided to remain silent. The concept that I would shoot him if he tried anything was implied by me pointing the shotgun at him.

Now what?

Now I supposed that I'd use the shotgun to my advantage and make *both* Malcolm and Allen stay where they were while I went inside and called the sheriff. If Malcolm couldn't keep his butcher knife out of Allen's throat, well, that wasn't my problem, but I wasn't willing to endure sleepless nights of guilt over this. No way. *Sorry, Malcolm, but nope. Next time you decide to murder a teenage kid, make sure he was really the one in the clown suit.*

Allen put out his arms as if trying to strangle me from a distance, then charged at me.

I assume he realized that, at this point, his life as he knew it was over. He'd probably realized it before he even ran away from the cabin. Why not go out in a big dramatic shotgun blast?

I couldn't pull the trigger.

Yeah, it was self-defense, but it was still killing somebody.

It was still the kind of thing that haunts you.

The kind of thing you can't ever get out of your mind.

Instead, I settled for using the shotgun like a club, smacking the son of a bitch with it as he reached me. I didn't really even need to swing it much—his momentum did most of the work.

Allen hit the ground.

That wasn't so difficult.

Malcolm came around the shed. He looked simultaneously relieved and angry to see Allen lying there, curled into the fetal position.

I didn't point the shotgun at Malcolm, but rather pointed it at the ground in a way that I hoped sent the message that I *could*, if I were so inclined, point it at him.

"We're calling the sheriff," I said.

Malcolm narrowed his eyes, as if he did indeed get the shotgun message. Then he looked down at Allen, whose eyes were squeezed shut and who was back to muttering under his breath. He might have been praying. I couldn't tell.

"If you insist," said Malcolm.

"Yeah, I do."

"Let's get him away from my daughter, then."

Malcolm reached down and grabbed Allen by the back of the collar. He tried to yank him to his feet, but the back of Allen's shirt tore. Malcolm grabbed him by the arm instead and pulled. Allen made no effort to stand up; he just lay there like dead weight.

"You're going to pull his arm out of its socket," I said.

"So?"

I supposed it didn't matter. "Why don't you go in and make the call?" I asked.

"No. I'm keeping an eye on him. You make the call."

"No. I'm keeping an eye on you."

"On me?"

"Yeah?"

"Why?" Malcolm asked.

"Why do you think?"

Malcolm shrugged. "All right. You're the boss." He tugged on Allen's arm again, then gave it a not-so-gentle twist. "Get up or I'll rip your arm off."

Allen kept his eyes closed, but stood up.

"You really messed up his face," Malcolm told me.

"I know."

"Nice work."

"It was self-defense."

"I didn't suggest that it wasn't. I'm just saying, nice work. Got him worse than he got you." Malcolm shoved Allen forward. "Though not worse than he got Rachel."

"This isn't about revenge."

"I didn't suggest that, either. You're really in the mood to put words in my mouth today, aren't you?"

With Malcolm's firm guidance on the back of his neck, we led

Allen to the front porch. Any day where your face gets slashed and burned is a terrible day, but I figured that things could have gone a lot worse. All things considered, it had worked out reasonably well.

Those were the exact words that went through my mind: *All things considered, it had worked out reasonably well.* I assumed that later that evening, as I lay in my motel room whimpering about how much my poor face hurt, I'd decide that things had *not* worked out reasonably well, but at the moment, with me not dead, Rachel not dead, Malcolm not a two-time murderer, and Allen in our custody, things seemed okay.

An instant later, I worried that I'd jinxed myself.

An instant after that, I discovered that to be true, assuming one believed in the ability to jinx oneself.

Allen went berserk.

It was difficult to attribute motives to the guy, but presumably he'd decided (again) that since he was screwed he might as well try whatever method he could. Or he'd been cleverly waiting to lull me into a false sense of security while I thought about how things had worked out all right.

Malcolm lost his grip, and though I smacked Allen in the chest with the barrel of the shotgun, it didn't stop him. He lunged at me, reaching for my eyes.

I hit him with the shotgun again, and he staggered toward Malcolm, who slammed the butcher knife deep into his chest.

Allen let out a soft squeak, almost a yip.

Malcolm wrenched the blade out of his chest. Then he grabbed Allen by the back of the neck and pulled him forward, while jamming the blade into his chest again.

Allen's mouth dropped open. A new trickle of blood dribbled over his bottom lip.

I took several steps back and dropped the shotgun. Holy Christ.

Malcolm pulled the knife out. He looked like he wanted to jab it in yet again, but then he noticed my horrified reaction. Though I don't know for certain what he was thinking, he seemed to consider that I'd write off the first stab as self-defense, and the second stab as making sure the job got done, but that a third stab could be construed as nothing but making the piece of shit suffer. That may have been projection on my part. He was probably just thinking, "*Die! Die! Die!*"

He let go of Allen. Somehow, Allen stood upright for a moment, before his knees buckled and he collapsed. My medical training went no further than CPR training in Cub Scouts (and even that was mostly spent making jokes about the dummy used for practicing mouth-to-mouth resuscitation) but it was abundantly clear that Allen would not be getting back up.

"Holy shit, Malcolm."

"He attacked us."

"I know, but holy shit, Malcolm."

"It had to be done."

"You could have let me hit him with the shotgun again."

"Clearly we do not see eye to eye on this issue. Now, if *I* were the one who'd just been mangled by him earlier today, I think I'd be more inclined to take my side."

Malcolm was surprisingly articulate right now, but his voice quivered and I noticed that both of his hands were trembling. In fact, he looked and sounded like he might be on the verge of tears.

He'd probably be more upset for me to see him cry than for me to see him kill somebody.

"I'm going in to call the sheriff," I said.

"Please don't."

"It was a clean kill." Well, far from *clean*, but he knew what I meant. "And now he's dead, so you don't have to worry about him blabbing about being the one who attacked Rachel."

"Then how do we explain why the hell he went after you? Why he went after her?"

"I don't know! Because he's a copycat!"

"It leaves too many unanswered questions."

"Look, I totally get that you're in self-preservation mode," I said. "I just can't be an accomplice."

"It's not about me," said Malcolm. "You have to think about Rachel. Think about what this would do to her. You say you care about her? Prove it."

"I do care about her. And I hate to be a dick, but I'm not convinced that you going away for a while would be such a bad thing for her."

"All right. I'm not going to try to convince you otherwise. But can we at least get Allen's body out of the way so she won't come out here and see it?"

"No. We cannot. That's evidence about what really happened. For God's sake, Malcolm, if you have Rachel's best interest at heart you can't do this! You're going to make things look worse than they really are! Accept what happened!"

Malcolm glanced at the shotgun on the ground.

Was he really going to go for the gun? Seriously? Is that where this was headed? I'd been through a lot today, and I really did not need to be wrestling around in the dirt with Malcolm over a shotgun.

"Don't do it," I told him.

"Don't do what?"

"You know what."

"Are we getting a little paranoid?"

"Are *we* getting paranoid? I don't even know what to..." I trailed off, deciding that this conversation was not worth having. "We're going inside. It's already suspicious that we haven't called this in."

He was still looking at the shotgun. When the hell was he going to quit looking at the shotgun?

Also, he was still holding the butcher knife. This could turn bad in so many ways.

"Like I said, you're the boss." Malcolm walked onto his front porch, leaving the shotgun behind. He paused in the doorway, then tossed the butcher knife over the rail and went inside.

I wished he hadn't actually tossed it away, since that was another thing that would look weird to the authorities, but I was extremely relieved that the gun and knife were no longer in play. Not that Malcolm didn't have more guns and knives.

I followed him into the house. Malcolm plopped down on the living room sofa, which is not where he needed to be if he wanted to make a phone call.

"Do you want me to call?" I asked.

"Do you really believe that this is the right thing to do? I think it's not. I think that we've been through enough, and there's no reason to drudge up old stuff. It doesn't help anyone. It won't bring peace to anyone. It'll just cause lawsuits and unwanted attention and a shitstorm that will ruin lives."

His voice cracked, and somehow I actually felt a little bad for him. Not bad enough to drag a dead body into the woods for burial in a shallow grave, but bad nevertheless.

Then he began to weep.

This was some awkward shit. One of the most chest-thumping macho men I'd ever met was sitting on his couch weeping. I think I would've been more comfortable if it was an all-out sob, something with a manly volume level, instead of these gentle tears with the occasional sniffle.

I just stood there, trying to decide if I should go make the phone call, or wait for him to regain his composure.

I lasted a couple of minutes before I couldn't take it anymore.

"I'm calling them," I said. "You go out and tell Rachel what happened so she doesn't walk out and see Allen's dead body."

"How about a bargain?" Malcolm asked. He sounded desperate and heartbroken.

"What do you mean?"

"We don't tell anyone what happened. You leave...and you can take Rachel with you."

"Excuse me?"

"I won't stand in your way. I'm pretty sure she loves you. We'll pack up her stuff, get her out of that damned shed, and you can take her back to Jacksonville. I'll wish you genuine happiness."

This was so bizarre that I had to stand there for a moment, trying to process what he'd said. "Let me get this straight," I said, flabbergasted. "You're saying that if I don't report Allen's death, I can bring Rachel home with me?"

Malcolm nodded.

"Like she's property?"

"No, not like property. This is what you wanted, right?"

"For her to move in with me?"

"Yes."

I could not believe what I was hearing. Suddenly Allen seemed like only the *second* most insane person I'd interacted with today.

"Okay, yeah, that's what we'll do," I said. "We'll hide Allen's corpse, clean up the blood, and pretend like we have no idea where he went. Then Rachel can grab a few of her owls, throw 'em in the trunk, and I'll drive her on back to live in wedded bliss with me. That'll work. That's a great bargain, Malcolm. You've got this all figured out, you fucking genius you. I've gotta say, anytime somebody gets stabbed to death with a butcher knife, I want you to be the brains of the operation, because nobody solves problems like Malcolm Kramer. This is especially great because now you don't have to threaten to kill me if I try to let somebody know about the dead guy in your yard! Yay for no more implied murder threats! Well done, sir. Well done. Yes, I accept your offer. I can't wait. Let's go tell Rachel right now."

Malcolm sat up straight. I thought he was preparing to stand up and kick my ass, so I braced myself.

But then, because apparently this *was* a goddamned farce, I turned around and saw Rachel standing in the doorway.

CHAPTER TWENTY-TWO

I don't know that much about physics, so I might be getting the science wrong when I say that, according to Einstein's Theory of Relativity, Rachel and I stared at each other for approximately ninety-seven hours.

Finally I spoke: "Okay," I said. Forty-three hours later (in Unbelievably Socially Awkward Situation Time) I followed that up with: "Yeah."

"Yeah," Rachel said.

"That whole thing I said was sarcasm."

"I got that."

"I'm sorry," I said.

"Why are you apologizing?"

"I don't know. I honestly don't know. This isn't a situation I've ever been in, or ever thought I'd be in, and no matter how much I try I can't come up with something to say that seems like something I should say in this situation." I was babbling, yes, but I felt no shame over this. If there was ever a time when it was justifiable that

I wouldn't be able to come up with a concise way to express my views on the matter at hand, this was it.

Malcolm didn't even get as far as babbling. He just sat there, looking like he had the worst case of food poisoning in recorded human history. I think he wanted to sob, puke, and then slash his wrists.

"Dad...?" Rachel said.

Malcolm didn't respond.

"Dad? It's really important that you talk to me right now."

Malcolm wiped his hands off on his jeans. He stood up, moving like an arthritic ninety year-old. "How much did you hear?" he asked.

"I heard you sell me to Jason in exchange for his silence."

Malcolm shook his head, although that seemed to take a lot of effort. "That's not accurate."

"It's simplified," Rachel admitted.

"It's him," said Malcolm, pointing to me. "Things were fine before he got here."

Why had this become a common theme? The way people were acting, you'd think I was breaking into the homes of Lake Gladys residents and taking a leak on their dining room tables while the family was saying grace.

"I thought you were trying to protect me all this time," said Rachel. "You were protecting yourself."

"That's not true. I love you. I'd do anything to keep you safe."

If I were Malcolm, I would've abandoned all pretense at dignity and just dropped to my knees, begging for forgiveness. I would've claimed temporary insanity. I would've started speaking in tongues to help shift the blame to Satan.

I wasn't enjoying Malcolm's struggle, yet I couldn't help but watch him in fascination, wondering how he was going to dig his way out of this deep, deep hole.

If I'd been watching Rachel more closely, I would've seen her take out the gun.

My mouth instantly went dry.

Malcolm closed his eyes and lowered his head.

Rachel pulled the trigger.

There wasn't as much blood and brain matter as I might have expected, though there was some of each. Malcolm dropped to the floor.

I lost all feeling in my legs, but somehow kept from collapsing.

Rachel lowered the gun.

"I need a few minutes to process this," she said, her voice hollow. "Do whatever you think you need to do."

She left.

I just stared at Malcolm's dead body, which lay on its side. A pool of blood was spreading under his skull.

Oh my God. Oh my God. Oh my freaking God.

I had no idea what to do.

My permanent facial scar was supposed to be my biggest problem of the day, but it kept getting eclipsed.

Should I call 911?

Of *course* I should call 911. Why would I consider, if even for a split second, not doing that? There was no other plan of action that made the slightest amount of sense except to go straight into that kitchen and pick up the phone.

Why the hell wasn't I walking into the kitchen?

Rachel hadn't murdered her father in cold blood, exactly, but it definitely wasn't self-defense, either. She might not get the death penalty, but she'd be going to prison for a long time, possibly the rest of her life.

I could testify on her behalf. Say that her dad had kept her in a shed. That he offered her to me to hide his own crime. You could pretty easily convince a jury that Malcolm was a terrible father.

But, ultimately, Malcolm was just an asshole. You weren't allowed to kill people for being assholes.

I needed to force myself to walk into the kitchen before I made the stunningly stupid decision to involve myself further in this mess. I was a successful cartoonist. I had a good life. I would have to be completely nuts to put it at risk to help Rachel.

Why the hell wasn't I in the kitchen?

I hurried out of the house. Rachel stood next to Allen's corpse.

Rachel looked at me and traced her index finger over her face. "So he's the one who did this to me?"

"Yeah."

"I thought it was Brandon. I had no reason to believe it wasn't."

"Before we go any further, would you do me a huge favor?"

"Anything."

"Drop the gun. Or just put it someplace else. Anywhere but your hand."

"You think I'll shoot you?"

"No. I'd just rather not have anybody waving around a gun right now. I'm stressed out enough."

Rachel dropped the gun. I flinched when it hit the ground, as if it might go off, though it didn't.

"Thank you."

"No problem."

"I wish you hadn't shot your dad," I told her.

"So do I."

"But it's done." I pointed to Allen. "He's done, too. It's all done. Now we just have to figure out what we're going to do about it."

"I guess that's up to you."

"No, it's up to both of us."

"We're in this together?"

"All I'm saying is that I haven't called anybody yet."

Rachel walked over to me. She reached for my face, tracing my cut without actually touching the wound. "This was Allen?"

"Yes."

"Was he trying to make you like me?"

"I guess so."

"That's really messed up."

"I agree."

"I'm sorry I involved you in this, Jason."

"It's all right."

"Could you catch me up on what happened?"

"Allen kidnapped me at gunpoint. Took me out to the cabin. Explained that he was the one in the clown suit. Your dad had murdered Brandon with a shovel and buried him in the woods. Allen slashed my face with a razor and burned me with a blowtorch. I got free. Raced him here. Sheriff Baker came. Your dad sent him away while I hid. Allen got here. Your dad stabbed him to death with a butcher knife. You shot your dad."

Rachel wiped a tear from her eye and gave me a smile that didn't look remotely sincere. "It sounds like things might be a little out of control."

"A little."

"Which stage of grief is denial?"

"The first one, I think." I counted on my fingers. "Denial, anger, bargaining, depression...um, one more. Acceptance."

"I feel like I'm going through the first three all at once," said Rachel. "But definitely denial."

"We need to figure out what to do," I said.

"What you need to do is leave. Just go. I mean, don't leave town and look suspicious, but go back to your motel. I'll call you when this is cleaned up. Unless you report the murder, which I completely would not blame you for doing."

"I'm going to help you."

"No."

"Yes, I am."

Rachel shook her head. "I can clean up my own mess. I'm not going to let you crawl into the sewer with me."

"I choose to crawl into the…" I decided that I didn't like her metaphor. "I choose to help you. My choice. I'm an adult, and I don't want to see you get locked up after you're finally free. Allen was a psychopath and your dad was a prick, and it would be easier for us if they were both still alive, but they're not, so we'll work with what we've got."

"I can't let you do this."

"Yeah, you can."

There would be another death on my conscience when Chuck found out about this, since his head would immediately explode. I had no idea what kind of exit strategy might work out (Rachel and I running off and living happily ever after?) but until I regained my sanity, I was going to help her.

"All right," said Rachel. "Then I'll let you."

"Any brilliant ideas?"

Rachel pointed to Allen. "We'll leave him untouched. Stick to the truth as much as possible. If we can get rid of Dad and his car, it all makes sense. He killed Allen and then fled because he knew that everybody would find out the secret about Brandon's death."

"Sheriff Baker knows about Brandon, too," I said. "So it's in his best interest for your dad *not* to be brought to justice. Holy crap, we might be okay!"

"What about your face?"

"Like you said, stick to the truth. We'll say that everything happened the way it really did, except that after he stabbed Allen, your dad got in his car and drove off. The only problem is that they can probably tell when Allen died, so they'll wonder why we didn't call right away."

"I begged you not to call anyone until Dad came back. I insisted that he wouldn't just leave me. You were completely against the idea, but I pleaded and pleaded with you, so you gave me one hour before you called it in."

I tried to figure out if there was a gaping hole in the story. There didn't seem to be one. "Are we turning into criminal masterminds?" I asked.

"I hope not."

"So the first thing we'll do is get your dad's body into his car, so we can dispose of both of them. I'll take care of that part."

"You're not doing that on your own."

"Well, it'll be upsetting for you to be that close to him. He doesn't look good."

"I'm the one who made him look that way. I'm anything but squeamish. If you move him by yourself, his body will slide across the floor and we'll have a much bigger mess to clean up."

"You're right, you're right. I'm just trying to spare you the gory parts."

"You don't need to spare me anything."

I went outside and opened the trunk to Malcolm's car so it would be ready. When I returned, Rachel had put a garbage bag over Malcolm's head to keep the blood from spilling while we moved him. She took his arms, I took his legs, and we lifted him and carried him toward the door.

Yes, I was officially carrying a dead body with the intention of hiding it from the authorities. I was queasy and mortified and scared, but I also felt like this was the right thing to do. Not many people would agree with me.

We got Malcolm outside and all the way into his trunk without any splattery mishaps. Rachel slammed the lid shut.

"You okay?" she asked me.

"Not really."

"Me either."

"Now what?" I asked. "What's a good hiding spot for a car with a corpse in the trunk?"

"There used to be a twenty-four hour grocery store about twenty miles away," said Rachel. "Obviously, I haven't been there in the past five years, but I assume it's still open. We could leave the car there temporarily until we figure out what to do with it."

"Do they have security cameras?"

"I don't know. I've never scoped the place out."

"If somebody finds the car, they could review the security video and see who left it there."

Rachel sighed. "A movie theater would have no reason to monitor the parking lot, right? Dad's car would be the only one left after the movies were all over, but would anybody care? Would the police be checking movie theater parking lots for him?"

"I wouldn't think so."

"That's what we'll do, then. Just for tonight. Tomorrow we'll figure out a more permanent solution. I'll drive his car, you drive yours, and we'll ride back together."

"Won't people notice you behind the wheel?" I asked.

"We'll take the back way, but yeah, that's a major problem. I could wear a mask, but other drivers would notice that even more than my face."

"My car has tinted windows," I said. "We could fling some mud on the windshield. When you stop at a traffic light, you can just pretend to be leaning over to pick up something."

"That works," said Rachel. "And I'll wear sunglasses."

We scrubbed down the living room as much as possible. Were we missing microscopic blood particles? Perhaps. But if we handled this correctly, there'd be no reason for the police to bring in their experts.

Then, because we had no mud handy, we mixed our own using dirt from the neighbor's driveway, and then smeared it on my car.

I scooped up Ignatz, gave Rachel my car keys, and my dog and I got into Malcolm's car.

And that, ladies and gentlemen, is how I found myself driving along a desolate back road with a dead body in the trunk.

CHAPTER TWENTY-THREE

What the hell am I doing? I asked myself approximately eighteen thousand times as I followed Rachel through the back roads of rural Georgia.

This was insane.

This was more than insane.

This was insane to the ninth or tenth power.

This was where I had to admit to myself that I was in love with Rachel.

What other possible explanation was there? I had a problem with people telling me what to do, which might explain why I'd wanted to stick around Lake Gladys after being threatened, but helping Rachel hide a murder didn't really involve a "You're not the boss of me!" attitude.

I was in love with her.

She was a killer.

But I probably would've shot Malcolm myself if I were her.

Well, that was pushing it. I was more of a "practical jokes taken too far" kind of guy. Though until I was hidden away in a shed for five years and then offered to a stranger, I couldn't be sure *how* I'd react.

I certainly wasn't shedding any tears for Malcolm. He wasn't the worst person I'd ever known, but if I were asked to compile a list of the Top People I'd Met Recently Who Deserved To Get Shot In The Head By Their Own Daughter, he would've taken the #1 spot.

This was insane.

There was nobody in the entire world I could call for insight whose reaction would be, "Yep, Jason, covering up this murder is the way for you to go. Excellent decision-making skills, sir!"

There was a dead freaking body in the trunk of the automobile I was driving.

Even Ignatz knew this was a bad idea, and he occasionally made judgment calls in favor of eating his own feces.

I should turn around.

Nah. Too late. I was wearing gloves, of course, but if the police really wanted to prove that I'd been driving this car, I was sure they could do it. Hell, my own dog was probably shedding on the seat, and I couldn't guarantee that I'd clean up all of the evidence. I was locked into this course of action, like it or not.

And, impossibly, I was veering more toward "like it" than "not."

Muddying up my car wasn't exactly a Professor Moriarty piece of criminal genius, but as far as I could tell (which, admittedly, wasn't very far) it was working. I supposed that my definition of it working was limited to not seeing any cars careening off the road. We could still be screwed.

When I reached the six-screen movie theater, I parked in the main lot, close to the building, where presumably no sane individual would park a car with a corpse in the trunk.

I put Ignatz's leash on him, then ran one of those sticky roller things you use on your clothes before a fancy night out over the seat to get rid of dog hair. Once I was satisfied that nobody would look inside and say "Be on the lookout for a guy with a Schnauzer!" I abandoned the car and walked Ignatz a couple of blocks to a grocery store, where Rachel was waiting in the passenger seat of my car.

I opened the back door, put Ignatz inside, then got into the driver's seat. "Done," I told Rachel. She sniffled and wiped her eyes. "You okay?"

Rachel nodded. "I guess I'm having an emotional reaction. Who knew?"

"And you're sure you want to go through with this, right?"

"I'm the one who should be asking you that."

"Hey, I'm feeling great. Expanding my skill set. There's not a lot of stability in the world of comic strips, so it's good to learn new things, just in case." I thought about what I'd just said. "Actually, that's not true. Having a successful comic strip is one of the most stable jobs in the world. Newspapers almost never trade them out. Strips run for decades, then when the creator dies, their kids take over. My comment about there not being stability was completely wrong. I apologize. Let's go."

Rachel had no response, since there was no need to respond to my nervous rambling. I started the engine and pulled out of the parking space.

We didn't talk during the entire drive back to her house. She cried much of the way, and I considered offering worthless platitudes like, "Everything is going to be okay," but why insult her intelligence?

I was filled with much less regret and self-loathing than I would have expected. Honestly, even though I knew I'd be haunted by images of blood spurting from the back of Malcolm's head, and though I'd be forever worried about the authorities breaking down my door, I didn't truly regret this. I felt worse about *not* feeling guilty than I did about hiding the murder.

I half-expected—well, fully expected—to see a dozen police cars in front of the house when we arrived, but no, it was just as we'd left it.

I parked and shut off the engine. "I guess we're pretty solidly committed to this now."

"Yeah."

"Are you going to be okay?" I asked.

"I feel like I'm going to have a breakdown."

"Go right ahead. I'll make the call."

SHERIFF BAKER STARED down at the dead body of Allen, looking ill. He reached for the walkie-talkie that was clipped to his belt, but I raised a hand.

"Wait," I said. "Let me tell you what happened before you call for backup."

"I beg your pardon?"

"This relates to...you know, the other thing."

"Mr. Tray, if you think I'm not going to call this in, you are out of your goddamned mind. But you've got one minute to tell me what happened."

"Malcolm beat the wrong teenager to death."

"Excuse me?"

I pointed to the corpse. "Allen's the one who attacked Rachel."

"How does a mistake like that happen?"

"Clown suit."

I told him the full story about my encounter with Allen, speaking very quickly. I went longer than a minute, but Baker didn't go for his walkie-talkie again. I took him through Allen's grisly death, and Malcolm's shameful bargaining attempt, and Rachel overhearing us.

Then we veered from the truth a bit.

"He just ran out of the house, got in his car, and drove off," I said. "Didn't take a suitcase or anything."

"Where do you think he went?" Baker asked.

"Not a clue. I couldn't tell if he was fleeing the state or really needed to get drunk."

"How long ago was this?"

"Hour and a half, maybe."

"*Hour and a half?*"

"That was me," said Rachel. "I begged Jason to give Dad time to come back on his own. I don't want Dad to go to jail. I don't want to go to jail myself."

"Why would you go to jail?"

"I identified the wrong attacker. It's my fault that Brandon's dead." Rachel began to cry. My first thought was, *wow, she's a fantastic actress*, but then I realized that her tears were genuine. She was legitimately distressed about her mistake. It wasn't a stupid mistake—I would've assumed it was Brandon in the clown suit, too —but the consequences were awful.

"Oh, now, don't worry about that," said Baker. "You're in no trouble."

"And Dad?"

"Well..." Baker looked down at Allen's corpse. "It was a brutal way to do it, but he was defending his own daughter on his own property. If the story checks out, this one was a justifiable kill."

"Brandon wasn't a justifiable kill," I said. "I hate to say this in front of Rachel, but it would be better for everyone if Malcolm never came back. I hope he's already long gone. At least he can start a new life in Canada or something."

"I hope you aren't suggesting that I not perform my elected job duties to the best of my ability," said Baker.

"I suggested nothing of the sort."

"We'll find Malcolm, and if justice needs to be served, it will be."

"I just want to say that I have no intention of saying a word about any knowledge you might have had about the incident five years ago," I assured him.

Baker narrowed his eyes. "Are you threatening me?"

"I'm doing the opposite of threatening you. I'm anti-threatening you. I'm explaining that my pledge of silence is still completely in effect."

I was being entirely truthful: no matter how things played out, I had no intention of telling anyone about Sheriff Baker's role in covering up Brandon's death. But I also felt that it might be useful to remind him that Malcolm's disappearance was a good thing, which might discourage him from using every resource at his disposal to find him.

Sheriff Baker stared at me for a moment, as if unsure what to think, then pulled his walkie-talkie off his belt and said he needed a couple of men dispatched to Malcolm Kramer's home.

THEY TOOK Rachel to the sheriff's department to give a statement and me to the hospital. The cauterization of the wound had not eliminated the need for stitches, so an elderly nurse sewed up my face while excitedly sharing how much her grandson loved Zep the Beetle. She put ointment on the burn, then taped some gauze over the whole ugly mess.

It might heal to something that I could live with, or there might be a skin graft in my future. Joy.

Then I was on my way to the sheriff's department to give my own statement. They recorded it with a video camera, and I gave the same "true except for the part where Rachel murdered her father" story that I'd given Baker.

I was told not to leave town.

Rachel met me outside, and we got into my car.

"How'd it go?" I asked.

Rachel held up her hands. "I'm not in cuffs."

"Well, that's good. I think it's going to be okay. It's in Sheriff Baker's best interest to keep this as quiet as possible. Our story makes sense. As long as nobody finds the car before we can hide it permanently, we're okay."

"And as long as nobody finds microscopic traces of Dad's blood in his living room."

"Right. There's that. But they'd only find that if they had reason to believe that a crime was committed inside the house. Allen died outside. We're in good shape. We're fine."

"You don't believe that."

"I believe it ninety-nine percent. That's a good percentage. Maybe ninety-eight. Still good. If you'd pointed the gun at him, and I said that you had a ninety-eight percent chance of getting away with it, you would've done it, right?"

"I'd like to believe that if I'd put *any* thought into it, I wouldn't have pulled the trigger. I wasn't calculating any odds at the time."

"All right. Fair enough. Now what? Want me to take you home?"

Rachel frowned. "I'd rather not go back yet. They're still investigating the crime scene, right?"

"Probably."

"I can't do it. I can't stay there tonight."

"Okay, that's fine."

"Do you think we could get a pizza and go back to your hotel room?"

"It's a motel."

"Same difference."

"Sorry. I get pedantic when I'm taken by surprise. Yeah, sure, I mean, yeah, if that's what you want. You mean to stay tonight?"

"Yes."

"It's not a double. Just the one bed."

"That's okay."

CHAPTER TWENTY-FOUR

We got an extra-large pizza with double pepperoni, double sausage, and extra cheese. Even if we were compatible in no other way, our pizza preferences were completely in synch.

Rachel and I sat on the bed, stuffing our faces and drinking caffeinated sugary carbonated beverages. I'd considered asking if she wanted to get a bottle of wine, but I didn't want to imply that I was trying to get her drunk. Also, I didn't want it to feel like we were toasting the death of her father.

She seemed tense, and kept bursting into tears without warning. I considered this a good thing. I'd be frightened for my personal safety if she were behaving like a robot. Each time she'd cry, I'd give her a hug, she'd apologize, I'd tell her there was nothing to apologize for, and then we'd return to pigging out.

We ate an alarming amount of pizza on that bed. Rachel was slender, but she could pack that stuff away. Ignatz had tried to join the party several times, but he'd finally been given a slice and now lay asleep in his doggy bed on the floor. When Rachel and I finished the entire pizza (including the toppings that fell off, though we did not lick the crumbs out of the box) I climbed off the bed and set the cardboard box on the dresser drawer.

"Where do we go from here?" I asked.

Rachel held up her left hand. "First, you're putting a ring on this finger if you want any play tonight."

"What?"

She laughed. "I'm kidding! Relax, Jason. Let's not worry about the future right now. The future is scary." She beckoned to me. "C'mere."

I walked over to the bed. She scooted over to the edge and leaned toward me, then pulled back. "No, wait, we had pepperoni. Let me brush my teeth first."

"We both had pepperoni."

"That's irrelevant." She got off the bed. "Back in a second."

"You don't have a toothbrush."

"Can I borrow yours? No, that's gross, sorry. I'll just swish some toothpaste around my mouth."

"I've got Scope."

"Even better. Be right back."

She hurried into the bathroom. I paced nervously for a few moments. We had not specifically said that we'd be having sex. Rachel might just want to cuddle. I definitely wasn't going to push it. I was cool with however far she wanted to take this tonight.

I'd never slept with a virgin. Tara, my first girlfriend, had *said* she was, but her vigor implied otherwise. I wasn't sure if there was anything special you were supposed to do. I'd never researched the subject. At thirty-eight years old, it was reasonable to assume that there was no deflowering on my agenda.

It would be okay. I knew how the parts worked.

I heard her gargle some mouthwash. It was not a particularly sexy gargle, but I was getting turned on anyway. The grisly violence of today seemed so long ago.

Dammit. Why had I thought about the grisly violence?

I needed to get those images out of my head. That's why Rachel and I were spending the night together: to create more pleasant images.

Rachel spat out the mouthwash, which was not a turn-on, and I heard her turn on the water. I figured she would come out of the bathroom right after that, but she didn't. Though I couldn't tell exactly what I was hearing, it sounded suspiciously like clothing being removed.

I sat down on the bed.

Yep, that was definitely a zipper.

I listened carefully as more clothes hit the floor.

I heard her taking deep breaths, as if psyching herself up.

Then she stepped out of the bathroom, completely naked.

I'd grown so accustomed to her disfigured appearance that I honestly hadn't thought much about the fact that all of the damage had been to her face. The rest of her was stunning.

She gave me a shy smile. "Hi."

"Hi."

"Some women are embarrassed by their bodies, but I think it's my best feature."

I had nothing clever to say. I was under breast hypnosis.

"Is it all right if we don't go all the way?" she asked.

"Of course."

"We'll have fun. I just decided I'm not quite ready for that."

"We can do whatever you want."

"May I invade you with the toothpaste tube?"

"No."

"I'm sorry, I should only be saying sexy things. In case you couldn't tell, I'm very nervous."

"I'm nervous, too," I said.

"No, you're not. You've had hundreds of women."

"I wish."

"Dozens, then."

"You understand that I draw a cartoon bug for a living, right?"

"Yes. I'm surprised we were able to get through the whole pizza without some other woman trying to mount you."

"Get over here."

"Do you want me to put a bag over my head first?"

"Stop it," I said. "Don't joke about that, okay?"

"Shouldn't we address the elephant in the room?"

"No. Screw the elephant. We're supposed to be enjoying ourselves."

"Okay. Well, I'm standing here all nekkid, and you're fully clothed, so you need to even things out."

"I can do that." I took off my socks and tossed them aside. Rachel watched me, smiling, as I peeled off my shirt. I was in pretty good shape by the standards of an almost middle-aged cartoonist, but, yeah, I was a little self-conscious. This was not the first time I'd eaten an alarming amount of pizza. I tossed the shirt aside and sucked in my gut.

"I hope you don't think you're done," said Rachel.

"No, ma'am." I stood up, unbuttoned my jeans, and unzipped my fly, being careful not to cause any damage to the monster that lurked beneath. (I did not use this phrasing out loud, nor did I think it at the time. It was neither a beast nor a micro-phallus. It was perfectly acceptable, and I felt neither shame nor undeserved pride.) I slid off my pants, making it very clear, if it wasn't already, that arousal was not a problem at the moment. I took off my underwear, and then we both stood there, completely naked.

"Is it rude for me to just stare at it?" Rachel asked.

"Do whatever makes you happy."

She walked over, put her arms around me, and kissed me.

We kissed for several minutes, until she not-so-gently shoved me onto the bed, where we kissed for several more minutes. And then we proceeded to do several other things to take our minds off our troubles.

With each new act, Rachel was hesitant at first, but once she decided she liked it, her enthusiasm was unsurpassed.

Afterward, still a virgin, Rachel lay with her head against my chest. "Thank you," she said. "That was a lot of fun."

"Thank *you*."

"You know, if Brandon hadn't behaved like a jerk, he would've gotten laid that night. I was totally ready to go through with it. If he weren't into mean practical jokes, we would've gotten to have sex and my face wouldn't be mangled. I don't think I'd ever have married him, but, God, my life would've been so much different."

I kissed the top of her head.

"I like that my life is going to be different now," she said. "I wish the circumstances weren't so extreme, but after five years I think I'm finally going to be happy."

"Me too," I said. "I mean, I was happy before, I don't want to imply that I was miserable, but now I'll be even happier."

"You're not going to dump me in the morning?"

"Nope. You're stuck with me until Ignatz decides that you're evil."

"What if they find out what I did?"

The pepperoni grease suddenly felt like it congealed in my stomach. "They won't."

"If they do, we'll tell them that you were helpless against my feminine wiles. I was like one of those mermaids who lure sailors to their death. You had no choice but to do as I say."

"That'll work."

"No, it won't. I'm grotesque."

"Knock it off."

"If we get caught, we'll tell them the complete truth. You won't get in much trouble. I did all of the really bad stuff."

"It doesn't matter, because we won't get caught."

"Okay."

"Since you've chosen to mess with our afterglow, what exactly did your dad say when you told him about us?"

"It didn't go well."

"I know that. But what did he say?"

"He said that you were a depraved pervert."

"Did he?"

"Yes."

"Because I had a romantic interest in his daughter?"

"Yep."

"No offense, but your dad sucked."

"He certainly did." Rachel snuggled against me more tightly. "I love you, Jason. You don't have to say it back."

"I love you, Rachel."

"I gave you permission not to say it back."

"I know."

"Can I ask you a question, if I promise not to be mad at your answer?"

"Sure."

"I swear I won't be mad."

"I believe you."

"Do you have a condom?"

"I think so." I knew I did. I hadn't packed them specifically for this trip, but I hadn't unpacked them after my last one.

"Good."

"Any special reason you're asking?"

"Don't worry, I'm not asking you to demonstrate superhuman endurance. Whenever you're ready."

"Give me ten minutes," I said.

"Okay."

"Eight if you keep doing that with your hand."

"I'm not doing anything. Ignatz, stop that!"

"Har har. I can see him on the floor."

"So you're a depraved pervert but not into bestiality. That's a relief."

"Now it's eleven minutes."

"I'll accept responsibility for that. Go get the condom."

I THOUGHT it went pretty damn well. I was gentle, we got through the process with no major blunders, and when it was over Rachel didn't say, "Well, *that* was a frickin' waste of time."

We held each other for a while, not saying much of anything. Then I got another condom, and we went at it like...well, not like wild animals or anything. I wasn't a superhuman sex machine. We were just a little more rambunctious this time.

I'm sure Rachel could have gone another round, but my time was over. If she woke me up in the middle of the night demanding that I satisfy her ravenous carnal urges, I could probably oblige, but for now my plan was to walk Ignatz and hope that my dreams were inspired more by the end of the day than that whole middle part.

"Remember, you have to come back," said Rachel, as I got dressed. "If I hear an engine revving and tires squealing, my feelings will be hurt."

"Should I leave the car keys?"

"Yes, please. Unless you were going to get us more condoms."

"We still have eight."

"Like I said, unless you were going to get us more condoms."

"Sure you're not a succubus?"

"I make no promises."

I attached Ignatz's leash to his collar, leaned over the bed and gave Rachel a kiss, then left the room.

I walked Ignatz to a grassy area outside and waited for him to do his business. Ignatz always seemed to relish the idea that I, ostensibly the master, had to stand around waiting for him to take a dump, and he sniffed around, in no particular hurry.

A large pickup truck pulled up next to us. It had been parked elsewhere in the motel's lot. There were four men in the back, but I only recognized two of them: Louie and Erik, my former buddies from Doug's Booze Wasteland. At least Holly wasn't there to encourage another fight. They jumped out of the truck.

"Still here, huh?" Louie asked, as the other two men, who looked Malcolm's age, also jumped out of the truck. All four of them had aluminum baseball bats. I didn't think they were inviting me to join their league.

"Yeah," I said. "Still here."

"That was a mistake." Louie strode toward me, holding his bat in the air as if ready to crack my skull.

I backed away. "Come on, Louie. This is ridiculous."

He took a swing at my head, but I was almost positive he missed on purpose. He was still just trying to intimidate me.

Ignatz barked at him. Unfortunately, a miniature Schnauzer did not produce the same level of intimidation as, say, a Rottweiler. One of the older men, a mostly bald, potbellied, sweaty guy who still looked damn scary with a baseball bat, also walked over to us.

Louie swung his bat again. He definitely wasn't trying to hit me. But as I stepped back, he dropped the bat and scooped Ignatz up into his arms. The other guy gave the leash a violent tug and the handle popped out of my hands. Ignatz let out a frightened squeal.

While Louie held him tight, the other guy grabbed Ignatz's front leg. "Make a wish."

CHAPTER TWENTY-FIVE

"If you hurt my dog, I will kill you," I said, trembling with rage and worry. "I don't care how many baseball bats you have, I will kill you. I don't care if you've got a shotgun in that truck, I will kill you. I will kill all of you. I will kick your fucking teeth out of your heads. I will rip your fucking chests open. I will break off your exposed ribs and stab you in the fucking eyeballs with them. I will scalp you with my bare hands; I'll just dig my fingernails underneath the skin and rip your scalps right off, and then I'll wad them into a fucking ball and shove them down your fucking throats so that you choke on your own fucking head-skin. I will break your fucking toes. I will break your fucking fingers. I will punch a hole in your fucking stomach. Do not hurt my dog. Put him down."

One of the other older men jumped out of the back of the truck. "I didn't come out here to hurt a dog."

"Me either," said Erik. "Hurting a dog is about as rotten as it gets. You know you're on the wrong side when you start threatening dogs."

The man let go of Ignatz's leg. "Yeah, I can see where they're coming from. The dog didn't do anything to anybody. He's not even trying to bite."

"All right, we won't hurt your dog," said Louie, setting Ignatz back on the ground. "I apologize for that. We all got a little worked up while we were waiting for you to come out." He picked up the baseball bat again and waved it at me. "But this doesn't mean that you're safe. It's time for you to leave town."

"I'd be happy to go!" I said. "The only reason I'm still here is that the sheriff told me not to leave! I hate this town!"

"What the hell is going on here?" asked Rachel, storming out of the motel room. She was, thank goodness, fully clothed.

Louie looked over at her, and his lip curled up in disgust. If he made some sort of comment about her face, I'd be forced to...stand there angrily, I suppose. I wasn't going to throw a punch at somebody who had a bunch of friends with baseball bats.

Rachel walked over to me. "Mr. Hastings? Mr. Clower? What are you doing here?"

Mr. Clower was the one who wanted to snap Ignatz like a wishbone. He looked at the ground. "A young man died today," he said.

"I know. Dad killed him."

"He wasn't a fine young man. He creeped most of us out. But we can't have citizens of our community getting murdered without there being consequences."

"The consequence being, we want you to get out of town," said Louie.

I tore the gauze off my face. "This is what Allen did to me!"

"Nobody is saying he wasn't a madman," said Mr. Clower. "His mom and dad raised him poorly. But people didn't get hacked to death before you showed up, regardless of their mental state."

I pointed to Rachel. "The whole thing with her happened five years before I got here! What is wrong with you people?"

Then I understood. Rachel knew Mr. Clower and Mr. Hastings because they'd been friends with her father.

"Were you guys there when Malcolm murdered Brandon Keaton?" I asked.

Mr. Clower looked away.

"We're not trying to dredge anything up, okay?" I said. "We're leaving. We're leaving now."

"Who's Malcolm?" Louie asked. "I thought Brandon ran away."

"He did," said Mr. Clower.

"No, he didn't," said Rachel. "You watched my dad kill him, and then you helped hide the body."

Louie looked confused. "What? There's a hidden body?"

"She doesn't know what she's talking about," said Mr. Clower.

"Yes, she does," I said. "I've never known a town that's worse at keeping secrets. Your town hall probably has a plaque to commemorate the occasion."

"This might be more than I wanted to get involved in," said Louie.

"How are you all even associated?" I asked.

"You made me look bad in front of Holly, so Erik and I decided to track you down. We figured you were shacking up with Blister, so we drove over there, but it was all blocked off with crime scene tape, so we figured you weren't in there, so—"

"He doesn't need the whole story," said Mr. Clower.

"I think it's relevant. We got there, and these guys showed up—"

"They showed up right after you got there?" I asked.

"Well, no, Erik and I smoked some weed first. I guess we were there for an hour or so."

"Maybe an hour and a half," said Erik.

"That long?"

"It was good weed."

"Yeah, you're right. Anyway, about an hour or an hour and a half later, these guys showed up. We asked what they were doing, and they said nothing, and we said we were there to scare you off, and they said they were there for the same reason, so we figured, hey, common purpose. We decided that if you weren't there, you were at a motel, and there aren't many motels in the area, so we found your car pretty easy. Then we just hung out in the parking lot and smoked some more weed."

"I smoked no weed," said Mr. Clower.

"You sure? I passed it to you."

"I'm sure."

"Your loss."

"You all just drove over together?" asked Rachel.

Louie shook his head and pointed. "Nah, we're parked over there."

"But you just happened to have enough baseball bats for everyone?" I asked.

"We're part of a league," said Mr. Clower. "We have mitts and caps in the back, too. Do you want to see?"

"No, I trust you."

The guy who'd been driving the pickup truck rolled down the window and leaned out. "Should I just park somewhere else? I thought this was going to be quick."

"We're almost done," said Mr. Clower. "Need anything else explained?"

"No, I think we get it," said Rachel.

"Then here's what's going to happen," said Mr. Clower. "We're going to escort you back home, and you're going to pack up whatever stuff you can't live without, and then both of you are going to leave town and never come back. Are we clear on that?"

I glanced at Rachel. My desire to not be bossed around was mitigated somewhat by the fact that I wanted to leave Lake Gladys anyway, and I was pretty sure that Rachel had no problems abandoning her shed.

"We're clear," she said.

"Good. Then it's all going to be easy."

I GOT MY STUFF—WHICH wasn't much, since most of it had burned in Chuck's cabin—out of the motel room and threw it into the trunk of my car. Then Rachel, Ignatz, and I drove toward her home, with the pickup truck and Louie's car following close behind.

"You don't have to leave," I told Rachel. "Technically we're not supposed to. We could tell Sheriff Baker about this."

"I'd like to leave. It actually sounds pretty great."

I reached over and took her hand, even though I was usually a "both hands on the wheel at all times" kind of driver. Instead of giving my hand a gentle squeeze, since it was still sore from Allen stomping on it, Rachel stroked my fingers.

"You can stay with me," I said. "It doesn't have to be permanent. Just until you find your own place. If you want your own place. If you don't, that's cool, too."

"Are you asking me to move in with you?"

"I'm saying that I won't kick you out, since you're suddenly homeless."

"We'll see how much we get on each other's nerves."

"Did I mention that your town sucks?"

"You did, and it does."

"And did I mention that I love you?"

"Yes. Three or four times while we were having sex."

"I love you."

"I have to believe you, because of all the shit our love has put you through. I swear I'm not high maintenance. You'll see." She smiled. "And I love you, too."

We arrived at her house and parked in front of the yellow crime scene tape. We were now adding another criminal act to our list, but this one was under duress, and I was pretty sure it was only a misdemeanor.

The other men parked as well. "You have ten minutes," Mr. Clower informed me.

Rachel and I ducked under the tape. "Is there anything you need from the main house?" I asked.

"Just a suitcase."

We went inside Malcolm's home and grabbed a couple of suitcases from his bedroom closet. Then we went over to Rachel's shed, where she put the open suitcases on her bed and began to throw clothes into them.

"What can I do?" I asked.

"Pack the owls."

I began to take the owl drawings off the wall. Would Rachel miss this place after she was gone? As far as I was concerned, we could fling a few Molotov cocktails in here and give it the same treatment as Chuck's cabin, but it wasn't as if Rachel had been chained to the wall. There might be a weird nostalgic element for her.

"They can't force you to leave everything behind," I said. "Once we get back and get settled, I'll hire a private investigator or somebody to come and collect everything else out of your dad's house."

"I don't want any of it."

"No, but we can at least sell it. I'm sure he's got some pictures and stuff that you want. We'll figure that out later; I just didn't want you to worry."

"Thank you."

There was a knock at the door.

"Has it been ten minutes?" Rachel asked.

"Those assholes wouldn't knock first." I went over and opened the door. Sheriff Baker stood there, looking extremely annoyed.

"Hello, Mr. Tray," he said.

"Hi."

"You're causing me a lot of headaches."

"We're not trespassing on a crime scene on purpose," I said. "They forced us to. They want us out of town. They were going to break my dog's leg."

"Seriously? They threatened your dog?"

"Yes!"

"That's not right."

"I know! There's something in the water supply or something. All Rachel and I want to do is be left alone. I know we're not supposed to leave town, but with your permission we'd like to get out of here. You've got my contact information. You can get a hold of me whenever you want."

Baker sighed. "I wish it were that easy."

"If we're not allowed to skip town, then you have to do something about those bozos out there. Give us twenty-four-hour protection. Does Lake Gladys have a safe house?"

"I'm afraid it doesn't."

"Then we're hanging out with you. Louie's pissed because I made him look like a jackass in front of his fiancé, and the other guys are scared that their involvement in Brandon's disappearance will be found out. Things are crazy. We need protection."

"That won't be an issue," said Baker. "I'm here because we know that Rachel killed her father."

CHAPTER TWENTY-SIX

"Oh," I said.

Rachel set down the owl figurine she'd been about to put into the suitcase.

"It's been a terrible day," said Baker. "I thought, what better way to unwind than by going to a movie? The Lake Gladys Cinema is closer, but they've only got the one screen, and the popcorn's better at the Banks. Do you see where I'm going with this?"

"Yes, sir," said Rachel.

"Bad luck," said Baker. "Both yours and mine. It's the kind of coincidence where you have to consider that maybe somebody upstairs is saying that you weren't meant to get away with it."

I cleared my throat. "So did you..."

"Yes, I opened the trunk."

"Oh."

"None of this was Jason's idea," said Rachel. "I threatened Jason at gunpoint to help me cover it up."

"I see. And then you threatened him at gunpoint to have sex with you in his motel room?"

Rachel considered that for a moment. "No. The sex was voluntary. How did you know about that?"

"The jackasses waiting outside couldn't wait to tell me that you went back to his motel."

"I'm sure they discussed it in a mature fashion," I said.

"Yeah, uh-huh, that's what happened."

"How did you know it was Rachel who shot him?" I asked.

"Lucky guess. She had a lot more reason to kill him than you did." Baker ran a hand through his hair. "All I wanted to do was enjoy some popcorn and watch a movie. That's not so much to ask out of life, is it?"

"You can still catch a later show," I said.

"Don't try to be funny."

"That wasn't funny. It was hopeful."

"Don't try to be hopeful."

"We were leaving town," I said, gesturing to the suitcases. "We'll be out of your hair. If you let us leave, this all goes away."

"Is that so? I have a dead body hacked up with a meat cleaver. I have another dead body missing part of its skull. You're suggesting that by letting you skip town, my headaches disappear? Is that your grand scheme?"

"It's not a perfect plan," I admitted.

"Do you know why I'm the sheriff of a small town like this? Because *nothing happens*. Because my ulcers are supposed to come from teenagers vandalizing street signs or drunks getting into barroom brawls. I'd love nothing more than for you to pack up your things and go, but I've practically got a lynch mob waiting out there. I can't keep this contained. I did something in the past that I'm not proud of, and now it's gotten away from me, and I have to accept the repercussions. Now are you going to come with me peacefully, or do I have to put you in handcuffs?"

"We'll come peacefully," said Rachel.

Rachel and I walked out of the shed, followed closely by Baker. Louie, Erik, Mr. Clower, Mr. Hastings, and the fifth guy whose name I didn't know were standing just outside the police tape.

"Go home!" Baker shouted at them.

"Where are you taking them?" asked Mr. Clower.

"Where do you think?"

"Are you arresting them?"

"I'm taking them in for questioning."

"Do you really think that's a good idea?"

"It's none of your concern if it's a good idea or not. Now clear out or I *will* start arresting people."

"How is this not my concern?" asked Mr. Clower. "You're making a huge mistake."

Rachel and I had stopped walking, but Baker prodded us forward.

"We can't let you do this," said Mr. Hastings.

"Are you fools seriously trying to obstruct me in the line of duty?" asked Baker. "It's like there's not a full brain between you."

"I'm just watching," said Louie.

"Well, stop watching. Go home. All of you. Now."

The men looked at each other, sort of sheepishly. Then they headed back toward their vehicles.

"Jesus Christ," Baker muttered. "I don't even want to live here anymore, much less be sheriff. Get moving."

Rachel and I resumed walking toward the tape. How much prison time was I looking at? Any? I hadn't killed anybody. Maybe I'd just get parole. Chuck's head would explode, but I could still draw *Off Balance*. It made me sick to think of Rachel escaping from one cell only to get thrown into another, but what could I do? Grab Baker's gun?

(I had no plans to go for Baker's gun.)

Rachel gasped and stopped walking. When I saw what she'd

gasped at, I stopped walking, too. The fifth man, the one whose name we didn't know, had reached into the back of his pickup truck and was now pointing a rifle at us.

"What the hell are you doing, Gene?" Baker demanded.

Louie, Erik, Mr. Clower, and Mr. Hastings all seemed to notice the rifle at once, and they all took several steps away from the truck.

"He doesn't represent us!" Mr. Clower insisted. "Nobody told him to do that! That's all him!"

"It's true!" Louie said. "I've never met him before tonight!"

Baker pulled his revolver out of the holster and pointed it at Gene. "Put the gun down, Gene."

The rifle wobbled in Gene's hands, as if he was wavering between lowering it or not. "But...but we were making them leave town!"

"Gene, lower the gun!" Baker shouted.

"Lower the gun, you dumbass!" said Mr. Clower. "What you're doing now is worse than what we were trying to hide!"

"I...I...I'm already in trouble, right?"

Rachel walked forward, moving with the confidence of somebody who was certain that the idiot with the rifle would not actually shoot her. He wasn't pointing it directly at her, but it wouldn't take much of an adjustment in aim for that to change.

"Rachel!" I called after her.

"He won't do anything," she said, not looking back. She walked up to the crime scene tape, ducked underneath it, and continued walking toward Gene. He looked confused and terrified; a man who'd made a ridiculous decision and wasn't sure how to fix it.

Surely she was right. Even somebody as demonstrably unintelligent as Gene would not murder a woman in front of six witnesses simply to hide his involvement in covering up a previous murder.

I just stood there, scared to make a sound or do anything that might startle Gene into squeezing the trigger.

"Lower the gun, Gene!" said Baker. "I won't tell you again!"

"Lower it, moron!" said Mr. Clower. "What the hell's the matter with you?"

I think Gene wanted to lower it, but he was paralyzed with thoughts of "*Oh shit, oh shit, oh shit, oh shit...*"

I held my breath as Rachel walked right up to him.

She yanked the gun out of his hands.

Gene quickly stepped away from her.

I breathed a sigh of relief. But Rachel didn't drop the rifle. She held it up and waved it back and forth. Baker pointed his revolver at her.

"I'm not pointing this at any of you!" she clarified. "You see that, right? Nobody is in danger of getting shot unless they make the first move! Do you see that, Sheriff Baker? I'm not specifically pointing this at anybody!"

"I see that."

"So don't shoot me!"

"Put the gun down, Ms. Kramer!"

Rachel shook her head.

"Do what he says!" I shouted. "You're gonna get shot!"

"I don't want to go to jail! I'd rather be a fugitive!"

"Yes, but you're gonna get *shot*!"

"Sheriff Baker won't shoot me! I'm not threatening anybody! The rifle is not pointed at any particular target! Everybody sees that!"

"Please don't shoot her," I told Baker. "She's just scared."

"Put down the gun, Rachel," said Baker, doing a remarkable job of keeping his voice calm. "This can be worked out."

Rachel took a step toward my car, which was about thirty feet away. "Jason, you don't have to come with me. But I do need your car, so I need you to throw me the car keys. I'm not stealing it. I'll make sure you get it back, I promise."

"No, no, I'm coming with you," I said. I wasn't really up for an exciting life of running from the law, but since this couldn't possibly end well, I didn't want her to flee on her own. I'd come with her and talk her into surrendering. Hopefully there'd be no hailstorm of bullets before we got to that point.

I headed for the tape. "You're not going to shoot me, right?" I asked Baker.

"That's correct."

"Thank you."

I ducked under the tape and joined Rachel.

"So, what, you're just going to let Blister get away?" asked Louie.

Rachel spun toward him, but pointed the barrel of the rifle at the ground. "Don't call me that! Don't you dare call me that! You want a scary local legend? I'll give you one! I'll be the scariest deformed creature any town has ever seen!"

It was too dark to see, but I think Louie wet himself. He glanced down at his crotch, looked pained and humiliated, and walked toward his car.

"Rachel, I'd like you to calm down," said Baker. "Everybody needs to stay calm, and we can work this out."

"I've already worked it out. Jason and I are leaving."

"I can't let that happen," said Baker.

"Yes, you can. You wouldn't be here alone if you'd told anybody what you found in the car. You're trying to keep this quiet. Well, guess what, if you let us leave, it stays quiet."

"It's not quiet! The whole damn town knows about it! People from the outside were analyzing the crime scene that we're illegally trampling all over right now! You don't know how hard we're working to stop this from becoming a media circus! It's not quiet!"

"Quieter, then. Less talk of the past."

Baker lowered his gun. "Go. Just go. I don't want to see anybody get hurt tonight. I'll be putting out an APB on the car, and you won't make it out of the state, but if you insist on waving around a rifle, fine, I'm going to end this standoff."

"Are you sure you want to do this?" I asked Rachel. A high-speed chase didn't sound appealing. Nor did plowing through a police barricade. Nor did any part of this, to be perfectly honest. This was going to get us killed.

"Yes," said Rachel. "It's better than prison."

"You might not go to prison."

"I bet I will."

"A jury might be sympathetic."

"No jury is *that* sympathetic."

"Plea bargain?"

"So I can get out when I'm eighty, and it doesn't matter what my face looks like?"

"Let's continue this discussion in the car," I said.

"Somebody needs to shoot that freak!" said Louie.

I don't know why, knowing that Rachel still had the gun, Louie would say something like that. Perhaps the shame of his wet pants was so intense that it further blurred his ability to discern "smart" from "really dumb."

Rachel just glared at him.

I opened my car door. Rachel started to walk to the other side, then hesitated. She walked back to me.

"Give me the keys," she said.

"Why?"

"Because you're not coming with me."

"What are you talking about?"

"I'm running away alone."

"The hell you are."

"I've ruined your life enough. If I let you come with me, I'm a horrible person. Give me the keys."

"Absolutely not."

Rachel raised the rifle, pointing it right at my face. "Give me the keys, Jason."

I dug the keys out of my pocket and held them out to her. The barrel of the rifle was too long for her to take the keys out of my hand while pointing it at me, so she lowered it for a moment and reached out. I could have tried to knock the rifle out of her hands, but that seemed like a good way to accidentally get shot. And if Rachel wanted to steal my car and flee from the law...well, I wasn't going to stop her.

Rachel took the keys, then pointed the rifle at me again.

"I'd really like to come with you," I said.

"You just want to talk me out of it."

"I'd like to discuss it, yes."

"Some other time, maybe." Rachel looked as if she were trying to hold back tears. "I..." She sighed. "Never mind."

I was almost positive she wanted to say, "I love you." I started to say, "I love you," back to her unfinished sentence, but decided that it was a terrible idea. Louie and the Dipshit Squad were already riled up. Why give them another reason to do something stupid?

"I'll see you later," I said.

Rachel shrugged. "Maybe."

She got into my car, closed the door, and started the engine. The rest of us watched as she drove away.

CHAPTER TWENTY-SEVEN

"You can't just let the freak get away!" Louie insisted. "What if she goes on some kind of murderous rampage or something?" He pointed accusingly at Baker. "That blood will be on your hands!"

"You're done talking," said Baker, walking over to the tape. "All of you, you're done! Go home. Do not say a single word about anything that has happened tonight. Not one word. If your family asks where your dumb asses have been, you say you've been out bowling. I've got cause to arrest every one of you, and I'll do it if I have to." He ducked under the tape. "I'm dead serious. Don't make me hunt you down. Clear out and wait for me to get in touch. Idiots."

The men reluctantly returned to their vehicles. Baker walked over to his car. "Get in," he told me.

I hurried over to the passenger side and got in. "We're going after her, right?" I asked.

"Yep."

Baker started the engine and peeled out of the driveway. He floored the gas pedal and I quickly buckled my seatbelt.

"If we can't catch up to her, I have to call this in and put out an APB," Baker told me. "I can't just let her go free without knowing where she's headed or what she's planning to do."

"I understand."

"But if we do catch her, and we can chat without those chuckleheads around, we might be able to work something out."

"Really?"

Baker didn't answer right away. "Want my prediction? This ends badly. She goes to prison for murdering her father. I lose my job and do some jail time. You do some jail time and people stop reading your strip. Shitty end for everyone."

"Let's talk about your bit of optimism."

"In a perfect world, those imbeciles will keep their mouths shut —which they might. They've got plenty to lose. In a perfect world, the story that Malcolm killed Allen and then skipped town is enough to explain why Malcolm isn't around any more. In a perfect world, we don't get caught getting rid of his car."

"Rachel and I were going to do that tomorrow," I said.

"Well, I'll do it better. Plenty that can go wrong, but if the glue holds those pieces together, we might get a happy ending for everyone except Allen and Malcolm."

"It seems too easy."

"Easy for *you*. I'm the one who has to clean this mess up. And none of it matters if we can't catch Rachel. That's too big of a loose end."

We reached our first intersection. A right turn led to town. A left turn led to...I had no idea. A dead end? Freedom for escaped murderesses?

Without asking my opinion on the matter, Baker turned right.

"Do you have any idea where she might go?" Baker asked. "Did you discuss any future plans?"

"Yeah, she was going to move in with me. At least for a while. But it's not like she would drive down to Jacksonville and look up my address. I have no clue where she'd go to get away from the cops, except to drive away as fast as she can. Are you sure we can't just wait for her to let me know where my car is?"

"We don't know when that will happen."

Baker was driving way too fast. I understood that driving fast was sort of the point of a high-speed pursuit, but it wouldn't help us end this nightmare if we plowed into a deer. I reached to buckle my seat belt, even though it was already buckled.

We were coming up quickly on another turn.

A car pulled into the intersection, preparing to turn onto our road. Baker's headlights illuminated the side of the car, which was extremely familiar.

"Is that—?" I started to ask.

My mind flashed through several things at once.

Yes, it was definitely my car.

Why had Rachel turned around?

Had she changed her mind?

Where was Ignatz?

I'd left Ignatz sleeping in my car.

She was bringing my dog back.

She was making a dangerous left turn.

Baker probably didn't do many high-speed chases.

We were going to hit her.

There was a moment where I seemed detached from everything.

The deafening crash.

The flying glass.

The jolt in my chest as I was thrown toward the dashboard.

The sight of Baker's head whipping forward so violently it looked like it might rip off.

And then I was right back to full awareness of pain and horror.

Baker lay against the steering wheel, eyes closed. He'd taken a lot of safety glass to the face. It wasn't until he gasped for breath that I knew he was still alive.

I fumbled with the button to release my seat belt. It took three or four tries, but then I got it. The buckle popped free. I reached for the door handle and was able to pull it open on my second try. I tumbled out of the car.

I threw up.

My vision was kind of blurry, so I couldn't clearly see the damage to my car, except that it was bad.

I reached for something to use to pull myself up. Missed. Managed to stand up on my own.

I stumbled toward my car, pausing to double over and throw up again.

Lots of steam. Lots of hissing. At least the car was right side up. It was facing the opposite direction, so I guess it spun around. It wasn't that far away. I could make it.

I felt something running down my neck. Blood? Yeah, had to be blood. Though my vision was blurred I knew it wasn't eyeball juice.

My right leg tried to give way beneath me but I wouldn't let it.

I made it to my car. All of the windows were shattered.

I could hear Ignatz whimpering in the back seat.

Rachel was still in the driver's seat. It was good. It meant she hadn't gone through the windshield and onto the crumpled front hood.

It was too dark to see her clearly, except that she wasn't moving.

When I focused on her, I could see the blood.

Lots of it.

I tried to open the door, but it was far too badly damaged. I kept jiggling the door handle for several seconds before I realized that this wasn't going to work.

The back door worked.

Ignatz jumped out. I could see glass and blood in his fur, but none of his legs were broken. He'd be okay.

I staggered around to the other side of the car. As I did so, I wiped my index finger over my face to see if maybe the wetness just came from tears, but, no, my finger was red.

I opened the passenger-side door.

"Rachel?" I asked.

Rachel did not answer me.

I leaned into the car.

She was a mess.

"Rachel?" I repeated. "Rachel? Please talk to me."

She couldn't talk to me. She wasn't even breathing.

"Rachel, you have to open your eyes," I pleaded. "You can't go out like this. It's not fair."

Should I try CPR? What if she had broken ribs? I could stab her in the lung, if that hadn't happened already.

"This sucks, Rachel. Don't end it like this."

Her right arm was obviously broken, so I reached across her body, getting blood all over my arm, and grabbed her left wrist. It was warm and slick with blood and I couldn't tell if there was a pulse or not.

"Anything?" asked Baker, startling me so badly that I actually screamed.

"I—I don't know. I don't think so."

Baker looked horrible. He wiped some blood out of his eyes. "I called it in. An ambulance will be here soon."

"Thank you."

I could take her and run.

I could drag Rachel out of the car, carry her in my arms, and run through the woods to freedom.

We'd live in a cabin, foraging for our own food. I didn't need restaurants or hot showers or *Off Balance*. Just me and Rachel and Ignatz, living off the grid.

Baker wouldn't stop me. What was he going to do, shoot me in the back?

I could do this.

I could really do this.

I could pull her out of the wreckage, jostling all of her broken bones, sending even more blood spewing from her wounds, breaking her neck, and carrying her gore-drenched corpse into the woods.

I'd kill her if I moved her.

There was no escape plan.

It was over.

"Please, just open your eyes," I said.

Then she did.

SHE SAID nothing while we waited for the ambulance. I kept telling her that everything was going to be okay. I'm sure she didn't believe it, and I sure as hell didn't believe it, but it was something to say.

I refused to leave until the paramedics got her out of the car and onto a stretcher. It took forever.

Then we went to the hospital.

Rachel went to intensive care.

After I got my injuries patched up, I went to jail.

EPILOGUE

I gnatz lived happily ever after.

The rest of the story is a bit cynical. I learned some things about myself and about life in general.

First, love makes you do some insane shit.

Second, when your agent is already furious at you, the phone call where you ask him to bail you out of jail is *extremely* unpleasant.

Third—and this is the one that's kind of cynical about society— if you're a successful cartoonist, you can afford a really good lawyer.

This lawyer may be able to convince a jury of your peers, and Rachel's peers, that a Mr. Malcolm Kramer, enraged by the fact that you brought the evil threat of Allen back into his daughter's life, attacked you. A really good lawyer could even convince this jury that Malcolm intended to kill you...or, at least, that Rachel was certain beyond a reasonable doubt that this was his intent.

Yes, she shot her dad in the head, but only to save her boyfriend's life.

The jury is inclined to sympathize with somebody who was kept a pseudo-prisoner by her father for five years after having her face savagely mutilated. That she's in a wheelchair (by the end of the trial she'll be physically able to switch to crutches, but her lawyer will discourage it) also helps.

So, yes, trying to hide the evidence of a murder is a bad thing to do. But we were desperate. And in love. And, c'mon, Zep the Beetle is a charming character. The guy who brings his adventures to life can't be a menace to society.

Oh, don't get me wrong, we were still found guilty.

And do you want to hear something weird? Rachel, the one who actually shot her dad, got no prison time. Just probation.

Me? I got sentenced to a minimum-security facility for my role in covering up the murder for which she only got probation. Our legal system is a bizarre one, kids.

Sheriff Baker resigned. He and the others who'd covered up Brandon's murder got a slap on the wrist. A *hard* slap on the wrist, but just a slap. We don't keep in touch.

So, anyway, let's talk about love.

Sometimes it means that you would die for each other.

Sometimes it means that a person drives you absolutely crazy but you can't imagine being with anybody else.

Sometimes it means that you'd follow them to the edge of the world, or that you'd wait for them forever.

I think it's something different.

Something less dramatic.

My definition of love?

You would wait for somebody for eight months (with good behavior).

And take care of their dog.

Rachel was waiting for me.

—The End—

ACKNOWLEDGMENTS

Thanks to the mighty Tod Clark, the mighty Lynne Hansen, the mighty Wendy Latham, the mighty Michael McBride, the mighty Jim Morey, the mighty Rhonda Rettig, the mighty Donna Fitzpatrick Stinson, the mighty Paul Synuria II, the mighty Tristan Thorne, and the mighty Matt Worthington with their mighty assistance on this novel.

BOOKS BY JEFF STRAND

The Writing Life: Reflections, Recollections, and a Lot of Cursing. A comedic (but entirely true) non-fiction book about surviving in a brutal business.

Candy Coated Madness - Another demented collection of gleefully macabre tales.

Autumn Bleeds Into Winter - A coming-of-age thriller set in Fairbanks, Alaska in 1979. Fourteen-year-old Curtis saw his best friend get abducted, and he's going to confront the man who did it.

The Odds - When invited to a game that offers a 99% chance of winning fifty thousand dollars, Ethan rejoices at the chance to recoup his gambling losses. But as the game continues, the odds constantly change, and the risks become progressively deadlier...

Allison. She can break your bones using her mind. And she's trying very hard not to hurt you.

Wolf Hunt 3. George, Lou, Ally, and Eugene are back in another werewolf-laden adventure.

Clowns Vs. Spiders. Choose your side!

My Pretties. A serial kidnapper may have met his match in the two young ladies who walk the city streets at night, using themselves as bait...

Five Novellas. A compilation of *Stalking You Now, An Apocalypse of Our Own, Faint of Heart, Kutter,* and *Facial.*

Ferocious. The creatures of the forest are dead...and hungry!

Bring Her Back. A tale of revenge and madness.

Sick House. A home invasion from beyond the grave.

Bang Up. A filthy comedic thriller. "You want to pay me to sleep with your wife?" is just the start of the story.

Cold Dead Hands. Ten people are trapped in a freezer during a terrorist attack on a grocery store.

How You Ruined My Life (Young Adult). Sixteen-year-old Rod has a pretty cool life until his cousin Blake moves in and slowly destroys everything he holds dear.

Everything Has Teeth. A third collection of short tales of horror and macabre comedy.

An Apocalypse of Our Own. Can the Friend Zone survive the end of the world?

Stranger Things Have Happened (Young Adult). Teenager Marcus Millian III is determined to be one of the greatest magicians who ever lived. Can he make a live shark disappear from a tank?

Cyclops Road. When newly widowed Evan Portin gives a woman named Harriett a ride out of town, she says she's on a cross-country journey to slay a Cyclops. Is she crazy, or...?

Blister. While on vacation, cartoonist Jason Tray meets the town legend, a hideously disfigured woman who lives in a shed.

The Greatest Zombie Movie Ever (Young Adult). Three best friends with more passion than talent try to make the ultimate zombie epic.

Kumquat. A road trip comedy about TV, hot dogs, death, and obscure fruit.

I Have a Bad Feeling About This (Young Adult). Geeky, non-athletic Henry Lambert is sent to survival camp, which is bad enough *before* the trio of murderous thugs show up.

Pressure. What if your best friend was a killer...and he wanted you to be just like him? Bram Stoker Award nominee for Best Novel.

Dweller. The lifetime story of a boy and his monster. Bram Stoker Award nominee for Best Novel.

A Bad Day For Voodoo. A young adult horror/comedy about why sticking pins in a voodoo doll of your history teacher isn't always the best idea. Bram Stoker Award nominee for Best Young Adult Novel.

Dead Clown Barbecue. A collection of demented stories about severed noses, ventriloquist dummies, giant-sized vampires, sibling stabbings, and lots of other messed-up stuff.

Dead Clown Barbecue Expansion Pack. A few more stories for those who couldn't get enough.

Wolf Hunt. Two thugs for hire. One beautiful woman. And one vicious frickin' werewolf.

Wolf Hunt 2. New wolf. Same George and Lou.

The Sinister Mr. Corpse. The feel-good zombie novel of the year.

Benjamin's Parasite. A rather disgusting action/horror/comedy about why getting infected with a ghastly parasite is unpleasant.

Fangboy. A dark and demented fairy tale for adults.

Facial. Greg has just killed the man he hired to kill one of his wife's many lovers. Greg's brother desperately needs a dead body. It's kind of related to the lion corpse that he found in his basement. This is the normal part of the story.

Kutter. A serial killer finds a Boston terrier, and it might just make him into a better person.

Faint of Heart. To get her kidnapped husband back, Melody has to relive her husband's nightmarish weekend, step-by-step...and survive.

Mandibles. Giant killer ants wreaking havoc in the big city!

Stalking You Now. A twisty-turny thriller soon to be the feature film *Mindy Has To Die.*

Graverobbers Wanted (No Experience Necessary). First in the Andrew Mayhem series.

Single White Psychopath Seeks Same. Second in the Andrew Mayhem series.

Casket For Sale (Only Used Once). Third in the Andrew Mayhem series.

Lost Homicidal Maniac (Answers to "Shirley"). Fourth in the Andrew Mayhem series.

Cemetery Closing (Everything Must Go). Fifth in the Andrew Mayhem series.

Suckers (with JA Konrath). Andrew Mayhem meets Harry McGlade. Which one will prove to be more incompetent?

Gleefully Macabre Tales. A collection of thirty-two demented tales. Bram Stoker Award nominee for Best Collection.

Elrod McBugle on the Loose. A comedy for kids (and adults who were warped as kids).

The Haunted Forest Tour (with Jim Moore). The greatest theme park attraction in the world! Take a completely safe ride through an actual haunted forest! Just hope that your tram doesn't break down, because this forest is PACKED with monsters...

Draculas (with JA Konrath, Blake Crouch, and F. Paul Wilson). An outbreak of feral vampires in a secluded hospital. This one isn't much like *Twilight*.

For information on all of these books, visit Jeff Strand's more-or-less official website at http://www.JeffStrand.com

Subscribe to Jeff Strand's free monthly newsletter (which includes a brand-new original short story in every issue) at http://eepurl.com/bpv5br

And remember:

Readers who leave reviews deserve great big hugs!

ABOUT THE AUTHOR

Follow Jeff's ridiculous musings here:

 facebook.com/JeffStrandAuthorFanPage
twitter.com/JeffStrand
instagram.com/jeffstrandauthor

Printed in Great Britain
by Amazon